GESHE JAMPA
A Warrior of Tibet

(Novel)

GESHE JAMPA
A Warrior of Tibet

(Novel)

Neerja Madhav

BLACK EAGLE BOOKS
Dublin, USA | Bhubaneswar, India

 BLACK EAGLE BOOKS

USA address:
7464 Wisdom Lane
Dublin, OH 43016

India address:
E/312, Trident Galaxy, Kalinga Nagar,
Bhubaneswar-751003, Odisha, India

E-mail: info@blackeaglebooks.org
Website: www.blackeaglebooks.org

First International Edition Published by
BLACK EAGLE BOOKS, 2025

GESHE JAMPA: A WARRIOR OF TIBET
by Neerja Madhav

Copyright © **Neerja Madhav**

Distribution in India by Pralek Prakashan

Cover & Interior Design: GRS Graphics

ISBN- 978-1-64560-708-3 (Paperback)
Library of Congress Control Number: 2025942483

Printed in the United States of America

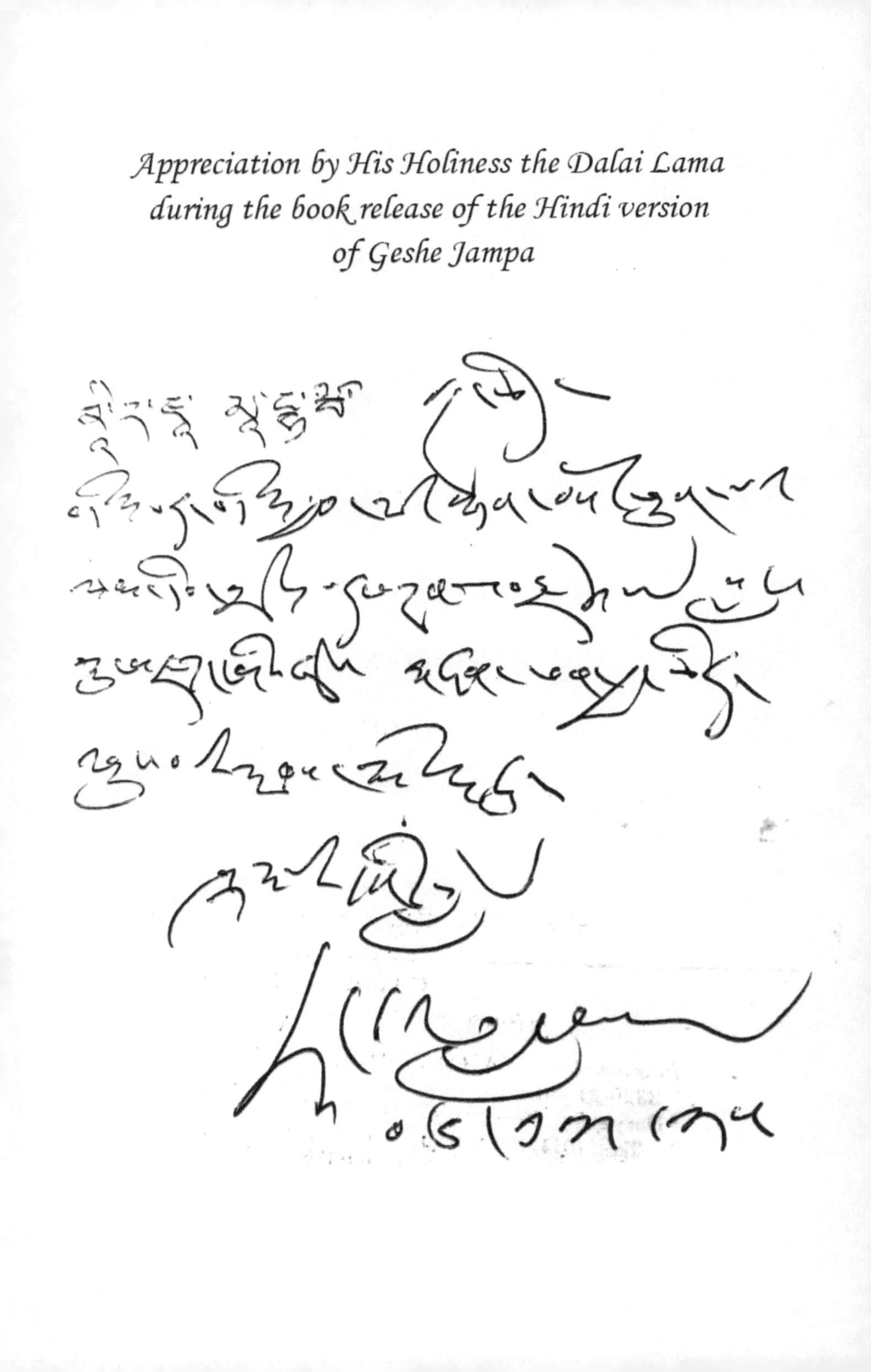

*Appreciation by His Holiness the Dalai Lama
during the book release of the Hindi version
of Geshe Jampa*

*To
the offended silence of
Tibet*

Truth Behind Writing

I found opportunity to see and listen to the Tibetan community around me living in Sarnath. In monk's clothes, in modern clothes, in traditional clothes too, roaming on the roads of Sarnath, moving in groups towards the Tibetan Bauddh Temple to participate in Kalchakra Pooja, involved in preserving their language and culture in monasteries and institutions or selling shawls and sweaters on the footpath in the winter season, these Tibetans are seen, associating themselves with Indian culture so firmly as river Yamuna meets with river Ganga but their separate identity has never disappeared.

Having an almost similar look in face-cutting and personality with our Laddakhi or Manipuri brothers and sisters of India, these Tibetans made me curious to know or write something about them once when I found a Tibetan lady as school teacher wearing a red-bordered white Saree[1] in the annual function of a children's school in Sarnath. She was singing the national-anthem of India. I was astonished and on that very day I felt once again the pleasure of Independence and grief of bondage and dependence.

There are a large number of Tibetans who are living in India but as refugees and on the other hand our relation with China comes in the way. A policy-matter that is going on for a long time. India does not consider the exiled-Government of Tibetans under the leadership of His Holiness the Dalai Lama situated in Dharmshala of Himachal Pradesh of India. India considers it only as their place of shelter as a matter of policy. A shelter to Tibetan refugees on humanitarian grounds. But whenever the fire of revolution

---

1. Saree- Traditional Indian dress.

enflammed in Tibet, the flame of the fire effected the relation of India and China also because the Tibetan community living in India is the biggest source of energy for Tibetan revolutionaries.

On the other hand, China and the exiled-government of Tibet have their own evidences and historical facts regarding Tibet on the basis of which they give the logic of their being true. But it is also a fact that in history, the relation of China and Tibet is found up to fifteen hundred years only. Till the last decade of 19th Century Tibet was free. Relations between China and Tibet were not heard of during the period. There were many struggles heard at the end of 19 century and in 1959 its climax was seen.

In this total episode India, having sympathetic attitude for Tibet too, never objected officially to the political attitude of China but considered it as an internal matter of China. This very policy was adopted almost by the other countries of the world too and in such a scenario on the other hand the Tibetans are constantly involved in their non-violent-freedom movement. Tibet is a country that has its own separate religious and cultural identity with its traditions faiths and rituals, in the crowd of the secular countries of the world. Tibetan movement is the only alive movement at present.

This novel is a small effort to break the silence on the issue of Tibetan's cultural and religious restlessness and their non-violent freedom movement.

A small hope is twinkling like a lamp while handing over this novel to you that perhaps..... .

Neerja Madhav

Madhuwan
SA 14/96 N-5
Sarangnath Colony
SARNATH, VARANASI-221007
Mob- 9792411451

1

It was a full moon night but the moon was veiled with fog. Sleep was far away from the eyes of Geshe Jampa. He was feeling restless. He threw himself in the easy chair. A group of ten children consisting of six girls and four boys aged between five to twelve years has been sent again to the monastery from Dharmashala today. In this severe winter, covering them with new and old woollen clothes, heaping one upon another the bundle of essential things with 'Jyupa'[1] and 'Masung'[2] on their back, their poor parents had driven them to the icy hills of the Himalaya stealthily so that they could lead a better life of peace in another country from the suffocating life of their own.

Geshe Jampa opened the window in restlessness. An immovable silence was scattered outside. A chilly gust tried to enter the room. He shivered when the cold air touched his naked arms piercing his shawl of catechu colour covering over the 'Cheevar'[3]. He tightened the grip of his hands firmly on his chest and looked outside. The silent and distant scenes were clearly visible from the low boundary-walls of the monastery. The mango, blackberry and tamarind trees were standing under the roof of mist across the road. The milky bulbs on the roadside poles were looking dim due to the misty weather. An unbreakable silence! It was only about ten o'clock in the night but the Roads of Sarnath seemed to be isolated due to cold.

A milkman was riding his bicycle. The silence of the atmosphere was broken. The bare buckets of milk were tied to the

---

1. Jyupa-flour from barley which is the staple food of Tibetans.
2. Masung-A kind of Tibetan cake made with black sugar, Ghee and Jyupa in milk.
3. Cheevar- A kind of dress of Buddhist monks.

handle and carrier both of his bicycle and were making a rattling noise with the speed of the bicycle. The silence was broken for a moment and the milkman moved ahead. The inner loneliness of Geshe Jampa was also interrupted for a while. He was reminded of something watching the shivering speed of the milkman. His attention was drawn towards the little guest who was sleeping in his room. Thinking that the little guest may feel cold, he shut the window with a heavy mood. The loneliness of the atmosphere was left outside. A state of confession and chaos had started in his mind. How long this chain would go on, he thought.

Little Tashi was sleeping in his bed. Aged about five or six years. He went beside Tashi's bed to cover him with a blanket. He changed the direction of the room-heater and moved it towards Tashi. An innocent sorrow was clearly visible on the face of little Tashi in deep sleep too. His heart was filled with extreme sympathy for Tashi. He sat on his bed and started stroking his short hair softly.

'cha-fu[1]......ma-fu[2]'

Tashi was murmuring in his sleep. Geshe Jampa's heart suddenly filled with extreme compassion for Tashi. Other children, came with Tashi had told him that after leaving Tibet and ascending the icy mounts their eatable things were finished. Tashi started to create troubles for them in climbing the hills. He wept bitterly calling his mother again and again. At that time, extreme cold was in favour of them because soldiers of the Indian border had gone to lower hills leaving their watch houses situated on the upper side of icy mountains empty, otherwise hearing the cry of Tashi, all of them would have been caught by the soldiers. They wanted to enter the Indian soil as soon as possible and by any means. Climbing the icy peaks of mountains, their tea-pot became empty. Tashi fainted demanding 'cha-fu, ma-fu' due to the excessive cold. They thought at first that perhaps he was no more

---

1. cha-fu-give me tea.
2. ma-fu-give me butter.

but Mangfe felt his slow breathing. In his unconscious state itself, they carried him on their backs one by one and came down from the height of hills to India.

'Mom ...... Mom.'

Perhaps Tashi was talking to his mother in dream. A sweet smile was spread over his face. His lips were contracting and expanding again and again in laughing style. A very slow sound of joy was coming out of his throat. Geshe Jampa's eyes were filled with tears. How this little boy has come to his lap leaving his parents, he thought. This separation from his parents will be intolerable for Tashi. How will he be able to make him understand this situation? He is so innocent. Since evening, Tashi was insistent to go to his mother and he would have to convince him somehow—

'O.K. Tashi, if you drink this milk and finish your meal, I promise to let you go to your mother."

'No, I'll go at once.' Again he persisted in Tibetan language.

Look Tashi, it is a dark night. No mule will be available in 'Sho-la'[1] . How will we move? If a dangerous Dong[2] comes in our way, what shall we do?

Geshe Jampa tried to frighten him talking about the dangerous path to his homeland. He succeeded in his aim. A dark shadow of fear spread over the face of Tashi.

Perhaps he was reminded of that gruesome journey of only a few days ago. He hastily concealed himself under the "Cheevar" of Geshe Jampa. He clung to him with his chest and it stroked his short hair slowly with affection.

'When will we go tomorrow?' Tashi asked Geshe Jampa peeping from his Cheevar like a tortoise.

'Only after taking lunch.' He tried to avoid him by his vague answer.

'But I'll not take this meal.'

"Then, what will you take?" His voice was affectionate.

---

1. Sho-la- A place of long ascending.
2. Dong- Wild animal

'Rice and meat of Chamri[1].' Tashi eagerly put his demand before him.

'Yes. Anything more?' At this time Geshe Jampa wanted to divert his attention anyhow.

'And…..and…..tea.' Thinking for a moment, Tashi replied.

'O.K. I'll bring everything in the morning. Now you go to Mangfe and Chhungchi and sleep with them.'

Taking Tashi down from his lap he suggested.

'No, I'll not go there. I'll sleep with you.'

'listen Tashi, Chhungchi will tell you a story there. You must sleep with her.'

He tried to make him understand.

'No, I have to sleep with you only. The night frightens me.' He whimpered. His eyes immediately filled with tears.

'O.K. come with me.' Geshe Jampa wondered whether Tashi would start weeping again, so he brought him to his room. The old lady monk Loye Dolma of this monastery was given the responsibility of arrangements for other children who came with Tashi.

Dolma was very caring and affectionate to the children who escaped from Tibet in hope of betterment.

In the beginning, this monastery was simply a Tibetan Buddhist temple, but as per need and seeing a huge number of Tibetan children as refugees, a centre of Bhot-culture and education was also established beside this monastery with the financial support of the Government of India. In this centre, the Tibetan children were being taught their own culture and language along with Indian languages, especially Hindi, so that they may not face any problem in day-to-day life and thus their own culture may also be protected through.

Lady-Monk Dolma was guardian of these children as well as the manager of this Buddhist temple too. Loye Dolma was deputed here long back before Geshe Jampa was appointed as chairman

---

1. Chamri-Wild race of deer.

of this institution. The teachers, workers and children of this institution had great respect for Dolma. In the beginning, Bachau, an Indian, started to address dolma as 'Maai'[1]. His tea stall was beside the monastery. Gradually she became 'Maai' for all Tibetan monks and girls and boys. She became popular as Maai in Sarnath. For Geshe Jampa she was as respected as his own mother.

'Mom'...' Tashi was trying to catch something in sleep raising his hands. The Smile of sometime before now turned into sobbing. He was weeping silently in dream.

Geshe Jampa held his hands that were raised in the air and softly caught them into his own hands. This gave a kind of solace to little Tashi and he then went into deep sleep.

How mother is a god-gift to human life who never let off a man from sleep to wakefulness, from womb to old age and door of death, she never leaves it alone. In memory or dream, pain or pleasure, in every moment mother stands with it, whether live or sublime. This time too, Tashi's mother was in his dream and Geshe Jampa's mother was in his reminiscences. His heart again fluttered remembering his mother. How will she be? In which condition? He has not received any whereabouts of his mother for so many years. All of a sudden, the frozen ice of reminiscences started to thaw and the dimmed picture of affection clearly appeared before him.

Mama wept bitterly clinging him to her chest the whole night. Her face was wet with tears. He himself has caught her tightly as if the devil was coming to snatch him from his mama. When the sobbing of mama gradually increased, he also plunged into an ocean of tears. Listening to the pathetic cry of mother and son his father woke up. He removed his 'Chuk-tu'[2] and set it aside on the bed and touched mama's arm gently. Mama's grief broke the walls of limit and her tears turned into an indistinct voice—

"I can't survive without Jampa. Please don't send him to India."

---

1. Maai-A local dialect for mother.
2. Chuk-tu-A kind of soft and warm blanket.

"Do you think that I can survive without him? You know the reason for which we have taken this decision to send him there. We are helpless." Father was also sobbing.

'No, I'll not send him. How will I survive? O God! What shall I do?' Mama's languid hands fell down on the pillow. Her emotional grief was in its extreme.

'Look, we are sending Jampa in order to save his life. Also, he is not going alone? The children of 'Lha-Dong'[1] and 'Chhu-shor-gy-pon'[2] village are also going with him.'

Father was trying to persuade mama but his own voice itself was full of emotion.

'Oh, Jampa's father! how I can prepare my heart to understand. How my little Jampa will climb the peak of 'Sho-la'[3] and 'Kharu-la'[4]? How will he cross Yum-dog-chho[5]?'

Sitting on the bed, mama was beating her chest out of extreme grief. He also sat rising from the bed and started weeping watching his mother's condition. Father had embraced both of them and had himself started sobbing. The minds had refused to think anything more and they were weeping bitterly clinging with each other.

Little Jampa had guessed a few days before that mama and father were deciding to send him somewhere. These days mama used to spread his woollen sweater and other clothes on the valley rocks in sun-light outside the home. Sometimes she used to take a cloth and inhale it whether they were dry or not. Doing all these, all the time her eyes were filled with tears. Jampa had an allergic tendency to woollen clothes kept for a long time in a box. He started sneezing from the smell of it. Watery discharge from his nose used to make his face red to the extent of sickness. So,

---

1. Lha-Dong-name of a village in Tibet.
2. Chhu-shor-gy-pon-name of a village in Tibet.
3. Sho-la-slopy and ascending peak of mountain in Tibet.
4. Kharu-la- --do---
5. Yum-dog-Chho-A huge and long pond situated on the top of hills, now almost dry in Tibet.

spreading his clothes and 'Chhupa'[1] in the sunlight was a regular practice of mama. The doctor had told her to do so. She always kept ready hot-tea with salt and scented pure butter in a thermos so that his problem may not increase.

'Mama, why do you pull out my clothes, from the box?' He was curious to know.

'Um…. Yes……'

She seemed unable to reply him and silently gazed at his face.

'What happened mama? Why don't you say anything?'

The Silence of mama exhibited itself in tears at his obstinacy.

'Why are you weeping mama? Are you reminded of Cho-cho[2] Kon-Chog?'

Mama moved her neck in refusal. She was unable to speak due to the flood of tears in her eyes. Her throat was choked and refused to utter a single word.

'Then, why are you weeping? Are you remembering aachaa[3] Chinye or 'Mag-pa'[4]?

Little Jampa was perplexed and asked frequently but no exact answer was found from mama due to her sobbing. Very often he saw his mother's solitary tears flowing for brother Kon-Chog and sister Chinye. Whenever she was alone, she put their old clothes in her lap and constantly used to weep whilst touching them softly.

That incident had happened only two or three years back. At that time, Jampa was about seven years old. He could remember his elder brother Kon-chog very well. Mag-pa generally used to be somewhere out of the house. Mag-pa's real name was Chhering but mama and father used to address him as Mag-pa, so listening to his parents, little Jampa also started to call him Mag-pa. Tall and slim Mag-pa was very affectionate to little Jampa. There was a big round brown mole near the right ear of Mag-pa and when he

---

1. Chhupa-A Tibetan dress.
2. Cho cho-Elder Brother.
3. Aachaa- Elder Sister.
4. Mag-pa-Son-in-law living in his in law's house.

talked, the mole vibrated to and fro. Little Jampa used to slip away from him in the beginning but gradually he became habitual to see it. That sign of Mag-pa was still in his memory. While reciting a story to Jampa, Mag-pa's soft smile and pearl-white teeth always fascinated him. Very often he asked—

'Mag-pa, who has made your teeth?

'My mama'. And Mag-pa became sad. Jampa had seen Mag-pa in melancholy whenever his parent's reference came. While he was on his visit to outside, Mama used to tell his story to brother Kon-chog, her elder son-

Mag-pa's father was making a Chheechhya'[1] but so many obstacles were coming in its construction. Then he took two vows before God of 'Chamdo'[2]—first, that he will paint the idol of Buddha in Chamdo-Vihar with golden colour and second, will give a feast to all 'Lamas'[3] in the campus of the presiding deity in the nearby Vihar. Chhering had married Chinaye by that time. After the completion of Chheechhya, the day when they were engaged in giving feast to Lamas in the Vihar, soldiers of China attacked that land and forcibly captured it. It happened near about 1950.

Chhering's parents were assassinated in that battle and after few days Chinye was also lost from sight. Chhering escaped anyhow and reached his in law's house. Since then he was with them as Mag-pa. but now his routine has been completely changed. He made an organization against the exploitation by China and he himself started leading that organization. Kon-chog also joined him because he could not forget his loving sister Chinye who disappeared due to Chinese exploitation. His emotions were boiling all the time.

People could know about their mutinous organization when many of them were arrested and kept in a jail by the Chinese government. Mag-pa escaped anyhow and left his land. Spies of the

---

1. Chheechhya-a pasturage.
2. Chamdo- name of a place in Tibet.
3. Lama-Monk- (Buddhist).

Police department were searching for the mutineers. Frightened families began sending their children to other countries especially in India, the neighbouring one, in order to save their lives.

'Mam sss…' Tashi started weeping in sleep all of sudden and woke up.

The past of Geshe Jampa stopped at once.

'Take sleep… take sleep son!'

Geshe Jampa tried his best to make him sleep by his soft stroking.

'No, I have to go to my mama. Mam sss….!' Tashi began weeping sulkily.

It was 11 O'clock at night and Tashi was constantly weeping. Feeling helpless to convince him, Geshe Jampa took him in his lap and moved towards Dolma's room.

'Maai, please, you take care of him. You can make him silent. He is weeping.' Handing-over Tashi to Dolma's lap, Geshe Jampa told, as she opened the door.

'What happened? He did not sleep yet?'

Dolma's eyes were sleepy.

'No, he was in deep sleep but awakened just now and started weeping. Perhaps he saw a dream.'

'Come Tashi…. My dear child. Come, I'll tell you a story. Will you listen?'

Taking him in her lap Dolma tried to divert his thoughts.

The sleep had disappeared from her eyes by now.

'No, I'll not listen. Send me to my mama…. to my mama. I shall sleep with her. Mam…'

Again he wept loudly. His eyes were red. His whole face seemed to be red due to constant watery discharge from eyes and nose both.

Hiding him in her 'Cheevar' Dolma told— 'Look outside Tashi, how misty the atmosphere is there. How can one see the path in this mist? It is too cold to move. Let the sun rise, then we shall move from here. O.K. Do you agree?'

'No, my mama⋯… I'll go.' Tashi tried to come down from her lap.

'Look Tashi, I am also your mother. Everybody calls me Maai. Look at me my son. I am just like your mother my dear son.'

Astonished Tashi looked at her face for a moment and forgot weeping for a while. In between Dolma diverted his attention towards next—

'When I came here Tashi, there was a huge yak in the forest of Sarnath…. So huge…'

Dolma sprang up slowly raising her hand over her head. Tashi was surprised and gazed at her with curiosity.

'Oh, very big… bigger than it.'

Again she sprang up. Tashi enjoyed this act of leaping. Wiping his wet nose on her shawl she again sprang up in telling the height of the yak. Tashi laughed softly. Dolma's laughter was double.

'Oye….oye….it is too cold outside, isn't Tashi? Come, let us run away to my room. There I'll tell you how tall that yak was. Come….oh ho….so cold my dear son.'

Hiding Tashi in her shawl she moved ahead and winked at Geshe Jampa to go to his room. Tashi was engaged with her and forgot weeping.

Geshe Jampa moved from there with slow steps and in a gloomy mood.

2

Lobjang, sitting on the footpath in front of Birla Dharmshala[1] in Sarnath[2] with her open sky shop of sweaters and shawls, was watching the tourists with hope. She was waiting for customers to buy her woollen shawls, sweaters and caps but all was in vain. It became evening from morning but the sale was almost zero at her shop. A lady from Varanasi city wandering without aim came to her shop at noon and started bargaining for a sweater for her ten year old son.

'It will cost rupees two hundred and twenty five only'. Lobjang told her about the price of sweater. She became hopeful.

'Hunh, so costly? At Godaulia[3] the shopkeeper was so eager to give the same sweater only in rupees one hundred and twenty five. Hundreds of shops are there.'

She told carelessly.

'Oh Madaamji,[4] that will be the work of machine. Look at it, I myself have knitted it. Please, have a glance.'

Lobjang was showing the loop-holes of the sweater.

'So what? The lady was not influenced.

'Madaamji, there is a difference between hand-knitted sweaters and those made by machine, as there is difference between the meal cooked at home and in the hotel.'

In order to convince that lady, Lobjang was giving useless logic.

---

1. Dharmshala-A house for pilgrims in India.
2   Sarnath-A place in india(the birth-place of buddhism)
3. Godaulia-A market of Varanasi city in India.
4. Madaamji-word for madam.

'If you want to give it in that price, give me. I am not in mood to listen Puraan[1] at present. I'll not give more than one hundred and fifty rupees.'

Giving her final decision, the lady stood up.

Lobjang felt hopeless and helpless. Making wet her dry lips by rubbing her tongue on it, she told in extinguished voice-

'It is first sale of the day madaamji. Since morning, it has not been begun yet, so I am giving it in your price.'

Lobjang crammed the sweater in a plastic bag and gave it to the lady.

The motorcycle of her elder son Pema stopped nearby. Raising her head, she looked upon him. She was counting the rupees given by that lady and could not see Pema.

'Maa, I have to present some gift to my computer teacher. Today his marriage-anniversary is being celebrated.' Standing up his motorcycle on its stand beside the footpath Pema explained his desire to Lobjang.

'Then…..?' She was somehow upset.

'What then? All the students are giving their contribution for any expensive gift. Every student has to give one hundred.' A kind of carelessness was floating in his voice.

'And if you don't go to that function?'

'How do you talk maa? Will I not fall down in their eyes tomorrow? And after all, I have to take my degree of computer or not?'

Keeping his hands in both pockets of his jeans, he laughed at the innocence of his mother.

'Pema, you are well aware of our family condition. Dava doesn't have his school uniform. His school-bag is also torn. It was the old-one of the previous year. There is no tenant in our house these days.'

Lobjang was repeating her pitiable condition before him. A fixed amount from the tenant was the main source of income

---

1. Puraan-Anicent Religious epic of India.

for the livelihood of her family, through which she was dragging her household anyhow. It was in favour that Lamaji had built a small house in this very colony in time otherwise….. Many other Tibetan families also colonized it. Fed-up with the narrow streets of Varanasi city several people purchased their lands in this colony also. Some of them started living after building their houses. So, this was a mixed colony of Indians and Tibetans.

Lama Sonam Dakpa, husband of Lobjang purchased that land in installments and gradually built three-four rooms. Now, when he was bed-ridden due to old age and sickness, Lobjang had given two rooms on rent and herself opened a cloth-shop on the footpath according to season household expenses were met anyhow. Pema was doing a computer course according to his own will. Ten years old Dava was enrolled in a primary Bhot-culture and educational centre. He was getting free education there. She also wanted to send Pema to the institute of Norbulinka[1] situated in Dharmashala[2] for higher Tibetan studies but he did not agree to leave Sarnath. Lobjang was upset by his behaviour.

Pema had gone after mercilessly taking one hundred rupees from Lobjang. Keeping the note of fifty rupees in the pocket of her Chhupa[3] she began to teach her younger son Dava who sat beside her on the footpath orally. In between the time her wandering eyes used to search for customers also, in hope-perhaps someone may come and she could sell some more articles.

'Sa means planet and in Hindi it means Nakshatra.'

She was teaching Dava. She was of the opinion that knowledge of Hindi and English languages are essential with Tibetan language. But the situation was to some extent reverse. Living with Indian

---

1. Norbulinka-A famous place in Tibet in which name an institute was founded in India also.
2. Dharmshala-Name of a place in India where exiled Government of Tibetan people works.
3. Chhupa-A dress of Tibetans worn on waist.

people the Tibetan children were well acquainted with Hindi but English and Tibetan language were to be taught.

'Why do we read English mama?' Dava asked innocently.

'So that, when you have to go to a foreign country, you may speak there.'

'And why do we learn Tibetan language?'

'So that, you can remember your own language.' Lobjang made him to understand.

'Is Hindi not our language?'

'No….. yes…… both are. But we are Tibetans, so……' Lobjang was confused by the questions of little Dava.

'Mama, shall we go to Tibet by learning Tibetan language?' Dava's curiosity was increasing.

'Yes….maybe… anytime.' She was lost in her thoughts.

'We'll leave our house here?... Goloo, our neighbour will also acompany us?'

'Oh, now you started wandering. See, learn it by heart. Sa-ni-ma-means Ravivar and in English it is called Sunday.'

'Sa-m-ma…. Mama, elder brother Pema will remain here?' Revising his lesson, Dava was still wandering in his realm.

'I don't know. Sa-da-va means Somvar and in English, it is Monday.'

Lobjang proceeded.

'My name is also Dava. Then I am also Monday?'

'No, you were born on Monday so your father gave this name.'

Oh yes. And on which day my friend Goloo was born mama?'

'My head. Your mind dances all over the world during study. Give me your exercise book. I'll write it down. Learn it by heart and recite to me tomorrow.'

And Lobjang started writing the names of days in Tibetan, English and Hindi languages in his exercise-book—

Sa-mik-mar-Tuesday in English   Mangalvar in Hindi.
Sa-lak-pa- Wednesday in English   Budhvar in Hindi.
Sa-fur-boo-Thursday in English   Guruvar in Hindi.

Sa-pa-Sang- Friday in English   *Shukrvar in Hindi.*
So-pen-pa- Saturday in English   *Shanivar in Hindi.*

'Mama several Tibetan children have come in my school. They can't talk to us. They talk only to Maai Dolma and Jampa Gela.'[1]

Dava informed her.

It stopped her pen from writing. She asked Dava "Where have they come from?"

'From Tibet. Maai told us. Our Hindi teacher Devyani Madam also repeated the same.'

'What?'

'Yes this much, that Tashi, Mangfe, Chhungchi, all will study with us. Tashi wept the whole night yesterday for his mama.'

'Oh, how old Tashi is?' There was a touch of sympathy in Lobjang's voice.

'Smaller than me. Up to here.'

Keeping his palm on his right shoulder, Dava explained the height of Tashi.

'Ch…Ch…Ch…Cha…. O Lord Tathagat…..'[2].

Folding both her hands in the style of salutation she bowed her head in front of the Buddha temple and picking up the goods, she instructed Dava to come with her.

Evening was darkening. The atmosphere was becoming misty. There was no hope of customers now. She wrapped up a big bundle of woollen clothes, put it on her back and moved ahead towards her home. Dava was going side by side holding her left hand finger. The striped Pangchhen[3] hanging over the black Chhupa was the evidence of her marriage. The long necklace of light blue pearl was swinging on her breast. The folded shawl was kept on her left shoulder. Her old sweater was visible from the loose sleeve of her blouse. She wrapped up her long hair and knotted it with a ribbon.

---

1. Gela- Sir.
2. Tathagat-A name of Gautam Buddha.
3. Pangchhen-A striped cloth that is the symbol of marriage of a Tibetan lady hanging over Chhupa on the waist.

Covering her head and ears with the printed silken scarf, she tied it under her chin.

'O sister Lobjang, Will you not buy an apple today for Lamaji?'

Ramdhari Patel's wife Fulawa asked her while she passed away from Fulawa's fruit-trolley at the crossroads of Sarnath.

'No Fulwa, it is…. In the house. Yesterday I had purchased and Lamaji did not eat.' Lobjang's answer was somehow hesistant.

'O Didi, please take it. Absolutely fresh. It has been purchased today itself from Paharia[1] market.'

Fulawa had shown her two red pomegranates which she held in her hands.

Lobjang stopped short and gazed at the pomegranates taking them in her hands.

'How much will you give them for?' she asked the price.

'O Didi,[2] have I ever bargained with you? For others, It's sale price is forty rupees per kg., but for you only, it is of thirty five.'

Lobjang thought about her fifty rupees kept in her pocket. She had to purchase potato, rice and tomato for her household. In frustration she put back the pomegranates on Fulawa's trolley and said—'Let it be now Fulawa. I'll buy it tomorrow.'

Fulawa guessed her helplesness. 'O Didi! you take it for him. Price will be given afterward. Neither you nor I, are going away from Sarnath.

Weighing one Kg. pomegranates Fulawa handed them over it to Lobjang. Lobjang took out the money from her pocket with hesitation and gave to Fulawa.

She had not borrowed anything from anyone in Sarnath till now. Her ego never permitted it. She was surviving with optimism. The day will come when their problems will be removed. This kind of optimism in her was not only for her family but also for her country Tibet where they could go back.

---

1. Paharia-Fruit Market in Varanasi city.
2. Didi-Elder sister.

Lobjang's first husband had run-away leaving her alone after the birth of Pema. Since then, she was struggling for herself as well as for her children's life. She was separated from her parents in very childhood and being helpless, she married old aged Tenzin. Tenzin her first husband, was serving as guard in a monastery at that time. To become in many eye-sights, Lobjang thought it better to be attached with someone so that she may be saved from the prurient eyes of so many persons. Tenzin was very cruel to her, but she tolerated everything, his drinking wine to physical torture also. She was residing with Tenzin in a hut built in the campus of the monastery. Sometimes, Sonam Dakpa, a monk of the monastery used to interrupt in the quarrel and, domestic violence between husband and wife. Sonam Dakpa was about thirty five to forty years old at that time. Lobjang was young girl of nineteen years old. Tenzin's first wife was no more. He was thirty years old at that time. When his first wife died and his only daughter became motherless, he again married to Lobjang in order to look after his daughter.

Very often he used to come late in the night in weariness of wine and start fighting with her. After the birth of Pema, one day he wrapped his bundle of clothes and went out without telling anything. He did not return. The burden of step-daughter Seering also came upon the head of poor Lobjang. In that crucial time Lama Sonam Dakpa had supported her.

Lost in her thoughts, when Lobjang reached the threshold of her house, the chain of thoughts was broken. She knocked at the door softly with her finger.

'Who is it?' A tired male voice came out from inside the house.

'Open the door Lamaji. It is me.'

'Oh, just coming.'

The door was opened in few moments. Sonam Dakpa stood in front of her. His spordic mixed hairs were knitted behind the head in the form of a pleat. His orange Cheevar was crushed. A small rosary of light green colour was wrapped round his right wrist. Covered in a shawl, the face of Sonam Dakpa looked pale.

'Do you feel unwell?' Standing on tip-toe she touched his forehead with her palm. The body of Sonam Dakpa was warm.

'No, it's O.K.' His voice was weak.

'Have you taken medicine?' Proceeding towards kitchen Lobjang asked him.

'No. Medicine of cough finished yesterday.'

'O God, I am just coming after buying it.' She began to search something in her old box.

'Don't go today. Bring it tomorrow, when you come back. Salt and hot water also will reduce my problem today.'

Lama Sonam Dakpa understood her problem. She was searching money in her box.

Lobjang had only fifteen rupees in her pocket after giving the price of pomegranates to Fulawa and with that money she had purchased one Kg. potato and one Kg. wheat flour. There was no money for medicine now.

'I have brought pomegranates for you, but its cool effect will increase your phlegm. You must take it tomorrow at noon. Doctor has advised to take at least one pomegranate per day because it enhances blood.'

There was child like innocence on Lobjang's face.

'Pema has not come yet?' Lama Sonam Dakpa asked.

'No, It will be night to come for him'. Lobjang was preparing tea for her husband. She gave a short answer. Dava put his bag on the rack built in the wall of the room.

'He has gone to the house of his Computer sir, by taking money from mama.' Dava gave information to his father Sonam Dakpa.

'Now, you sound like a radio.'

Lobjang rebuked him.

'Why do you give money to him? He may adopt wrong-way. His friends never seemed trustworthy to me.' Sonam Dakpa's voice was depressed.

'How long I'll follow him. He is quite grown up now. He himself can differentiate between correct and incorrect. Whatever may be,

I support him on my part. Further, may God Avalokiteshwarji[1] know.'

She was also upset somehow. Bringing three cups of tea, Lobjang sat on a small wickerwork cot nearby Sonam Dakpa's bed.

'Please, take your tea and don't worry. Too many worries may increase your illness.'

'He is roaming here and there without any thought for his family condition. You make him to understand.'

'O.K. you feel well first, then entangle yourself in other worries.'

Holding her cup of tea in one hand, she rubbed Sonam Dakpa's feet softly with the other hand.

She was again lost in her past for a few moments. She had to touch these very feet of Sonam Dakpa when she arranged the marriage of her step-daughter Seering with Tanchu Dhondhap. She had not much more gifts to give them except two pairs of clothes. The salary received from monastery for brooming-sweeping and wiping the floor was insufficient for their day to day necessities also. Anyhow she was feeding Pema and Seering in that salary.

A night before the marriage of Seering with Tanchu Dhondhap, Lama Sonam Dakpa came to her small hutment saying—

'Lobjang, keep it for your daughter. Give her as gift.'

A big briefcase was with him. She was overwhelmed by his kindness. She bent at the feet of Lamaji and touched them with her forehead. Right from that day her respect for him was boundless, and side by side a kind of attachment for her entered into the heart of hearts of Lama Sonam Dakpa too.

One day he went to senior Lamaji of monastery and made request— 'Gela, I want to marry. I think, it has become necessary for me.'

Gela had permitted him at once because there was no rigidity in Mahayaan.[2]

---

1. *God.*
2. Mahayaan-A sect of Buddhism.

'Go ahead and adopt married life. But always remember that you have not to forget your ultimate aim.'

'Yes Gela.' And in front of idol of Lord Buddha, he accepted Lobjang as his wife.

'What do you think Lobjang?' Sipping his tea, Sonam Dakpa stroked her, and suddenly she came back to her present.

'I think, how situations have been changed in these fifteen-sixteen years only. Perhaps my shadow itself is not lucky for anyone.'

She was frustrated.

'Why do you think so? Sorrow and sickness are always attacked to human life. And moreover, I became fifty five years old from forty years in between.'

He tried to laugh.

'Sirrah! I am also forty.'

As Lobjang told her age, Dava interrupted.

'I am also ten years old and read in class third.'

'O yes, you are the oldest creature of our family.'

Lama Sonam Dakpa laughed at him.

'Oh, I forgot to tell. Devyani madam, the Hindi teacher in Dava's school, had come. She wants to take two rooms on rent. Someone has given our address.' Sonam Dakpa informed her. Without spending a single moment she refused 'Acquainted persons should not be made tenants. Sometimes good relations are spoiled. And moreover, she is Dava's madam also.'

'Oh, only one formula cannot be applied everywhere. She is an educated woman. Throughout the day she will remain in her institution. Her mother and a brother only will live in the house. The doors of both rooms are towards the main gate. There will be no connection between us. She is in a Government job, so rent will be paid timely....that is why I wanted.'

Lama Sonam Dakpa made her to understand the whole thing. The proposal seemed to be O.K. to Lobjang so she also agreed.

'What does Madaam's brother do?'

She became doubtful.

'Perhaps, he is in job somewhere. Unmarried still.'

Sonam Dakpa explained.

'It will be better to ask Pema also,'

Lobjang proposed.

'Why will he object? Yet, if you want to ask him, no problem.'

Lama Sonam did not have the feeling of stepson for Pema. Dava was his own son but he was equally affectionate to Pema also. It was also because of Lobjang, as he could not see her depressed. Although Pema's behaviour was being harsh and intolerable towards him and Lobjang day by day.

'No need to ask him. We shall make Madam Our tenant.'

Lobjang also thought it unnecessary to ask Pema and she moved towards the kitchen with empty cups in her hands.

3

Devyani was teaching the geographical situation of Tibet to the students of Poorv-Madhyama[1] in the class—

'Tibet is situated on the highest place in the whole world, that is why it is called the roof of the world. What is it called?'

'Roof of the world.' The Collective voice of the students buzzed.

'Well done! China is situated to the east of Tibet and India and Nepal in the south. Russia is situated in the north and Iran in the west. Now, tell me, which country is south of Tibet?'

'India and Nepal.' The students spoke loudly with zeal.

'Very good children! you learn very quickly. Now, let us know about the rivers and lakes. The river Brahmaputra emerging from the east of Tibet meets with Tachhok-Khabab[2] and Kyuchhu[3] river that comes out from southern Lhasa[4] merges in the Hind Ocean going through India. In the same way, Maja-Khabab[5] merges in the Hind ocean joining the pious River Ganga in India via Nepal. Senge-Khabab[6] passing through Laddakh and Kashmir in India meets with Arabian ocean. There are so many lakes, lagoons and ponds in Tibet. The biggest among them is Namchho-Chhumo lake. Tell me, what is the name of that lake?'

Devyani again asked the students.

Geshe Jampa stopped for a moment outside the class room hearing the voice of Devyani. He had marked a positive change among the students, since Devyani has started teaching in this

---

1. Poorv Madhyam-An educational course in India equivalent to Xth Class.
2. Tachhok-Khabab-Name of a river in Tibet.
3. Kyucchu-Name of a river in Tibet.
4. Lhasa-Name of city in Tibet.
5. Maja-Khabab-Name of another river in Tibet.
6. Senge-Khabab-Name of a river in Tibet.

centre. Now they were taking interest in study, while before her arrival, they usually missed the classes with the pretence of a headache and other problems and remained in their rooms in the monastery. A new kind of enthusiasm took place for study among the students. They used to sit happily in Devyani's classroom.

Devyani was selected by the committee as a Hindi teacher having the additional ability in Tibetan language too. She was given preference for this post because in bachelor's standard she opted geography and political science also as her subjects.

'Now, let's know some other important aspects. Tibet is considered as a spiritual land of Aryans. The mountain Kailash Mansarovar, which is famous as the residing place of reverent deity Lord Shiva of Hindus, is situated in this very country. The Tibetan people, being Buddhist, accept trees, water etc. like deities. Thus, their religious observances are almost very close to our Vedic religion, where the whole of Nature is the manifestation of the ultimate power, the Par-Brahma.

'Is it Devyani? Really we are so close?' A tender silent question raised its head the heart of Geshe Jampa. Various sweet meanings surrounded this question softly. He detached his mind forcibly that was roaming in this sweet valley like a fawn and moved ahead having a hasty glance on Devyani, teaching in the classroom. Devyani was absolutely unaware of his presence outside the classroom. Holding an open text-book in her hands, she was looking at the students. She had worn a yellow cotton Saree,[1] and her long black, and straight hair were scattered on her waist. Her piquant beauty of copper-colour and large black eyes applied with cllyrium were an enhancing attraction of her gentle personality. Perhaps Devyani was well acquainted of these peculiarities of her personality that is why, she always used to uplift these qualities during make-up. Without any other artificial cosmetics, her simple beauty used to glitter.

---

1. Saree-A traditional dress worn by Indian woman.

'Gela, Tashi-Delek!'[1] Devyani saluted Geshe Jampa from the class-room itself when she saw him passing by. Bending his head slightly, Geshe Jampa accepted her salutation and gave response too. Once again his eyes wandered-over the face of Devyani in this process. Her face was now in front of him. An innocent smile was playing on her face in the posture of salutation. Her pearl white teeth were slightly opened with her smile.

Geshe Jampa bowed his head again after accepting her salutation and moved with speedy steps. He was feeling guilt on the weak emotions raised into his heart for Devyani. He started repeating his 'Mantra' silently on his rosary caught in hand—

'Oum Manipadme Hum......'[2]

He was muttering the hymn by heart and his footsteps were moving ahead to the room of Maai Dolma. It was necessary to know about the children who had come from Dharmshala. These children were knowing nothing except their own Tibetan language. To live here they must know Hindi. Devyani can teach them well. But she must have to spare time for it. Probably she would like to come before ten o' clock in the morning. In the evening…. but till that time, other teachers and employees of the Institute are gone. Only the children residing in monastery, Maai Dolma and he himself used to remain there. Will Devyani agree to it?

A stirring of thoughts began in his mind again. Her two periods in the morning can be lessened. It can be given to Naveen Sharma and Balendu Thapaliyal, one period to each. Thus Devyani will not be over-burdened.

Contemplating about the period he reached in front of Dolma's room.

'Maai, what are you doing.'

Hearing the calm and slow voice of Geshe Jampa Dolma replied from inside the room—

---

1. Tashi-Delek-Salutation in Tibetan language.
2. A hymn.

'Please, come in Gela…come. Tashi and Chhungchi are also here.'

Pushing the curtain of the door, he entered. Tashi was in Dolma's lap and his arms were around her neck. About twelve years old Chhungchi was constantly watching the face of Maai Dolma sitting beside him on the bed. Throwing a hasty glance at Geshe Jampa, Tashi again penetrated his eyes on the face of Maai Dolma.

The story telling is going on Gela!' Offering him seat, Dolma said.

'Well….well'.

He sat on the chair.

'Then? What happened further?' Tashi interrupted Dolma. Chhungchi also sat becoming alert to listen.

'You complete their story Maai.' Geshe Jampa smiled.

'Yes, then poor Chang Saichhyo went ahead riding upon his mule. Passing on the way, one day he saw a few children who were dragging a mouse tied with a rope round its neck. The mouse was trembling out of fear. Chang Saichhyo felt pity and he liberated the mouse, from the children giving his own bedsheet.'

Dolma was telling the story in their own Tibetan language. Tashi was listening attentively.

'Then, what happened?'

'Then… going after some way Saichhyo saw that a few children were training a monkey by whipping. He again felt pity for monkey. He gave his second bedsheet to the children and making the monkey free from them, he left the monkey in forest.'

'Hun'. Chhungchi was jolting her head.

' A few steps ahead, Saichhyo met some other children who were beating a bear with a stick. He gave his mule to these children and liberated the bear and left it near the mountain. Now he had nothing. He became a beggar.'

'Then, further…?' asked Tashi.

'One day, an officer gave him punishment knowing him as a beggar that he must be wrapped up in a leather of ox and thrown to the river. Poor Chang Saichhyo floating in the river, reached on its bank. There was that very mouse whom he made free from children. The mouse bit the leather and Saichhyo came out.'

'Hun.'

'At the same time, the bear and monkey also came there and they gave him a gift of oval shape that was glittering.'

'Then'? Tashi was out of himself.

'Then….innocent Chang Saichhyo prayed before that rare glittering object. Suddently, there appeared a big palace before him. Fruit trees and flowers also appeared surrounding that palace. Everything was present there. Chang Saichhyo began to live there with comfort.'

'Then, what happened again?'

Tashi's curiosity was at its climax.

'That is all. Now story finished.' Dolma shook her hands.

'One more'

Tashi demanded.

'Sirrah! no me lord! I'll die.'

She clapped to entertain them.

'Maai, your services can't be forgotten by the people of Tibet.'

Watching her affection for the children, Geshe Jampa's emotions sprang out.

'What service Gela? Only I make my frustrated time pleasant amidst these children. Real services are being done by you Gela.'

An affectionate look showered on Geshe Jampa by Dolma. She was observing Geshe Jampa and her fingers were stroking the hairs of Tashi.

'No Maai, your contribution can't be ignored and never will be. It is your humility and greatness also that you don't recognize it. You are the second mother of these children otherwise, how could they survive here?'

'It is their trust in us that they send their beloved iris-like sons and daughters struggling on the icy hills for a better life to India across the mountains.'

The eyes of old Dolma were filled with tears. She grasped Chhungchi also with her other hand.

'Yes Maai, we are the big support of the Tibetan people living yet in Tibet. They consider us as their power. The strugglers, against sub dual administration there, have deep faith in Tibetan people who are living in India. We are their energy and to save this energy, people like you are contributing constantly.'

There was a great regard in the eyes of Geshe Jampa for Maai Dolma.

'It is being heard that imprisonment and assassination of Tibetan agitators who are agitating against colonization by China is still going on.'

Worried eyes of Dolma focused on the picture of Lord Buddha hanging on the wall—

'Yes Maai, millions of Tibetan freedom-fighters are imprisoned till now. Earlier, in Tibetan monasteries, where there were more than eight thousand monks, now they are countable on fingers. Religious preachings are also restricted there.'

Geshe Jampa was saddened.

'Several countries of the world also have sympathy with we Tibetans, as Indian people and government both have co-operated with us sympathetically but in lack of joint co-operation, each and every year is passing away in expectation itself. God knows, when that time and year will come? These old eyes will be able to see it or not?'

Dolma was telling saying nostalgically.

Often, Geshe Jampa used to come to Maai Domla's room in his distressed moments and had discussion with her about the past and future of his country.

'Gela, Will we never be able to return our home?' Chhungchi asked all of sudden. For a long time, she was seriously listening the dialogue between Dolma and Geshe Jampa.

'Why, who told you?' Geshe Jampa asked Chhungchi in Tibetan.

'That…Lama Migmar who resides in the next room… he was telling.' Chhungchi was hesitant to disclose his name.

'What was he saying?'

'He was saying that once whosoever comes from Tibet, he never goes back there… But when I was coming from Tibet, my father told me that I will go back again when I am grown-up. Shall I not go back Gela?'

She was asking and her throat was obstructed due to tears. A shadow of fear was floating on the face of Tashi. He burst out—

'I shall go to my mama. Ma… Maa…' He began weeping.

'You will certainly go, son! One day, we must go to Tibet….We will go my son! We shall celebrate Losar[1] there with zeal. We shall eat a variety of Tibetan foods and ramble on the hills.'

Dolma tried to divert him. Chhungchi was not assured. She added—

'Lama Migmar was saying that when he was very small and coming from Tibet with his parents, they all were caught by the soldiers on the border of Nepal. His parents were imprisoned and his two elder brothers and he himself was sent with a guide. His parents could not come till now. We don't know whether they are alive or not? Gela, my parents also might be arrested and kept in jail? With whom will my little sister Pempa be living?'

Frightened Chhungchi started weeping. Tashi and Chhungchi both looked afraid.

'Maai, you instruct all the boys, girls and monks that they must not talk like this.'

Geshe Jampa gave an instruction.

'But Gela, how can one be stopped from remembering his or her past?'

Dolma's voice was distressed.

'I am not so cruel Maai that restricting them from talking about their family members or own country, but such type of discussions may cause frustration in their hearts. Our struggle will cool down.

1. *Losar-Tibetan New Year.*

Teach them to control their emotions. Good times may come any moment. Very soon also, after many years also or may be…'.

'No, no third sentence Gela. I can't hear it. I am performing penance for a long time after coming to this country. I can't see its fruitlessness Gela.'

Dolma interrupted Geshe Jampa in a sad voice.

'Now, we repent Maai that is why Tibet also had not established its diplomatic relations with all countries of the world, as other countries had done? Free Tibet had adopted the policy of keeping itself aloof from other countries. Today we are suffering the bad result of the same. Our agitation against the exploitation of 1959 could not be supported throughout the world.'

There was a deep frustration in his voice. His eyes seemed to relive the past.

'Actually the Tibetan population was completely of religious observance. Political awareness was less in them. After that exploitation also some countries used to recognize it as the internal matter of China and Tibet and none had become conscious. The situation became worse and everything was delayed.'

Dolma was in deep melancholy.

'We will constantly continue our non-violent movement and thus try to express truth before the world. Certainly we will succeed some day in our Mukti-Sadhna[1].

"I do say Gela that we don't have objection, if the whole world is converted into one nation. We are not segregatists, as our race and culture are safe in it. We would not have felt insulted in subordination of China itself if we were-treated as human beings and our language, culture and traditions were safe. But we are devoid of minimum human rights and requirements. For this reason also there is no way out except revolution for freedom.

The lady monk Dolma was excited to some extent.

"Truth can't be suppressed forever and this is the base of our Mukti-Sadhna.'

---

1. *Mukti Sadhna- A Hindi term of freedom movement.*

Geshe Jampa stood up to go. His steps moved out slowly. There was a divine peace floating on his face.

One edge of his dark red shawl was hanging down and touching the floor as if it were taking the foot-dust of a great accomplisher Geshe Jampa. The sun at noon was giving its sweet and soft warmth to the creatures. The solitariness of the campus of the monastery was interrupted by the chirping of the birds on the Peepal-Tree.

$$4$$

With a splashing sound the boatsman stopped the boat nearby a sandy plain across the river Ganga in front of Panchganga Ghat. Keeping the oar for support of the boat he jumped and stood in the water up to his heels and helped them to come down catching the rope of the boat. Pema, coming down from the boat with his friends, on the out spreading sandy plain was keeping his alert steps.

'Sir, should I stay?' The boatsman asked humbly.

'Oye, rascal! Shall we cross the river by swimming while returning? We have fixed you for both side, isn't it?'

'Oh sir, please kick on my back but not on my stomach. How it can be possible in forty rupees for both sides?' The boatsman requested.

'Then, we should give forty thousand?'

Pema's friend Dolkar growled. His eyes were red out of anger.

'No sir, how can I claim such standard? Only give me eighty rupees....'

'How old is your boat?' Pema questioned—

'Ten years.'

'How many passengers do you get per day?' The boatsman was perplexed. When Dolkar asked such question, Pema and his three friends Dolkar, Fungchung and Sheetal Patel looked like novices of these days. Bearing loose jeans and shirt like hippies, their hair was long like ladies and in the same way, they were having a shining ear-ring in only one ear. There was a small rosary of pearl on one wrist and a watch on the other of Pema. Fungchung has also worn such type of absurd dress. Only by their face-cutting and fair complexion they looked different from Sheetal Patel. Observing the Cheevar and shawl of orange colour of Dolkar, boatsmen thought him to be a saint, and it came into his mind that perhaps they have come to see the beauty of Ganga and Varanasi city from this side of river. It was quite a common thing because very frequently tourists use to come this side of Ganga and sit for a long time on the sandy plain.

"Is Gangaji your paternal property that you are charging so high? Ten years ago you have purchased this boat and rowing it this and that side. Now your calculation has been completed. You are robbing the public."

Sheetal Patel also growled in support of his friends.

The boatsman was frightened somehow.

'Move yaar! don't upset your mood. We shall give you fifty.'

Fungchung tried to subside the matter. The boatsman silently sat on his boat. They went away on the sandy Plain.

The sun was setting. All of them walked a while and sat on the sand. The fogy shadow of evening was peeping behind the trees.

'Dear, this is a very nice place. Why have we not come earlier?'

Pema was observing around him. A kind of silence was everywhere. One or two couples of lovers were sitting here and there and seemed like a shadow in the darkness.

'See there sir, Laila and Majanu![1] These boys and girls come to study in the University and come here with their lovers for merry making. They all are students of the University. Their parents have sent them to study and they are studying the lesson of love here.'

Sheetal Patel was rubbing his chest out of jealousy.

'Oh come on Sheetal, you remained what you are, a mere vendor of saltish fried food. All the time you are flowing saliva watching salty objects.'

Fungchung commented on him. All of them laughed loudly.

'You also removed your Cheevar for the same cause sir.'

Sheetal also reacted.

'There is freedom in our community that we can take off Cheevar anytime and accept family life.'

---

1. Laila Majanu-A famous lovers.

Fungchung put the logic.

'Sirrah! you can see Pema's father Lamaji.'

Sheetal brought out a piece of folded paper from his pocket. Everybody watched that folded paper with eagerness.

'Today, we shall take a puff, friends.' Pema told with eagerness. He had not minded Sheetal's comment about his father.

'Oh, when do you not take? It was yesterday evening when you took in Sarnath lawn…!

Pema interrupted the dialogue of Dolkar in the middle and said— 'Oh, that leaf-technique does not give amusement, friend, One will catch it, another will kindle fire, then a third can take puff of it.'

'That is why I brought you here. The enjoyment of this place is something else. It was very hard to search it out.'

Sheetal was folding another piece of paper in the shape of a cigarette keeping something in it of brown colour. Dolkar and Pema helped him.

'This place is safe also. Untill the police will cross the river, the people will take a bath in Ganga.'

Fungchung laughed. His dialogue was allegorical. Now, there was one cigarette in the hands of each and they were smoking.

'Exactly so, our police is very alert.'

There was an irony in what Sheetal said.

'Poor policemen, sometimes they themselves are caught red-handed supplying heroin, brown sugar, opium etc. to the prisoners.'

Dolkar laughed and coughed due to smoke.

'What about in your Tibet sir?'

Sheetal was out of control due to intoxication.

'Yes, I can tell you only whatever I have read through books. How I can know the situation of Tibet, as my parents came to India in my childhood.'

The eyes of Dolkar were becoming reddish. His mind was blowing with the wind.

'Sirrah dear! If you will try to know the whereabouts of your country, then you can know? You are living here in freedom and enjoying life, then who bothers about Tibet?'

Sheetal was teasing them.

'When the big lords are also lying idle here and there, then why we should worry. Has a dog bitten me that I should go there barking?'

Fungchung replied throwing his hand to the wind.

'O dear Fungchung, don't try to go there, otherwise they will sterilize you and you will remain single Fungchung. None will be there to help you.'

Pema made him alert in his stuttering voice. All of them laughed loudly. Intoxication overpowered them gradually.

'You are right Pema. I have also read somewhere that the whole villages were sterilized by the Chinese exploiters in Tibet. They forcibly make conjugal relation with the Tibetan ladies and produce their own race.'

Fungchung expressed his bookish knowledge.

'Are your Tibetan ladies factories that they produce children for them?'

Pema stood up out of anger at this odd comment of Sheetal.

'Sheetal, you are making ugly comments about our ladies. This will not be tolerated.'

'When you were talking like this, then nothing happened and when I repeated the same, you took otherwise?'

Sheetal protested.

'No, your intention was not good.'

Pema's voice was slurring due to intoxication. He was trembling while standing. The burning Cigarette between his fingers was glittering in the darkness.

'Oh dear! sit down. You are increasing a quarrel unnecessarily. It matters little. It is the tradition of our Tibet that there is a single wife of many brothers, so that property may not be divided. Now, how can you deny this fact Pema?'

Dolkar tried to make him understand and sat down holding his hand.

'No, his intention was not good.'

Pema was repeating the same sentence as he was intoxicated.

'Leave it Pema. Most of the males become Lama.'

Fungchung turned the topic.

'That is why Tibet is facing such hardship. Either they became Lamas or there was single wife for the whole male members of the family. How many children can be produced by a poor single lady?'

Dolkar pretended to be serious. His cigarette was damped. Throwing it away on the sand, he gave his opinion.

'I have heard that there in Tibet, the Lamas are very much respected. Their urine is also used with meal of parched grain. It is just like a boon.'

Sheetal explained with pleasure.

'Shi….sh…..sh…..please be silent. None should listen. Don't speak rubbish about us.'

Keeping his finger on lips, Dolkar forbade Sheetal.

'No, his intention was not good.'

Pema was repeating the same. Meanwhile, he watched Sheetal with an angry eye.

'That is why I removed my Cheevar Pema. You also remove Dolkar for the same reason. You also…… we shall produce many children. We will increase our population.'

Fungchung started weeping out of intoxication. After few moments he laid down on the sand by weeping.

'If you have to increase your population, please go to your country. Don't increase here in India. Don't snatch our livelihood here by increasing your population. Will our own children go to your country in search of a job?'

Now Sheetal Patel started speaking.

'Sheetal, this is not proper behaviour with the guests. We Tibetans are your guests. We have not come to do any work here. We are just guests of your country. You should not behave like this.'

Dolkar tried to make Sheetal understand politely. His voice too was slurring.

'You see Sheetal, now, if you want to send us back there, try to think, who will understand our Hindi, the Indian language, there in Tibet? We know Tibetan language very little. Yes, think over, what we will do there? None will understand our language.'

Fungchung also tried to make Sheetal Patel understand with blowing mind.

'The Chinese soldiers are camping there. They have captured schools, offices and everywhere. Where will Tibetans get jobs? Neither we are safe there, nor we can inhale free air. If some one opposes, he is being captured and imprisoned.'

Dolkar was explaining still. He was disclosing the truth of Tibet in the condition of intoxication. The emotions were coming out of their inner selves.

'You think over it Sheetal, the small boys also are snatched out and admitted in Chinese Force. Parents are shot dead. How we can produce children by going there? You yourself must think Sheetal.'

Laying on the sand Fungchung was telling.

'No, his intention is not good.'

Pema was murmuring.

'No, you have to go back, Fungchung. I shall not let you to put your trolley also beside my trolley of salty snacks. I'll give-up my life, but won't allow you to snatch the livelihood of my children. You keep it in your mind.'

Sheetal began to sob slowly. In few moments, a silence spread out there on the sandy plain. They slept in full effect of intoxication.

The boatsman came nearby and called them slowly out of fear, but there was no reply from that side. He went back to his boat and after few moments the splashing sound of the moving boat broke the silence of sandy plain of Ganga. Boatsman was going back towards Panchganga Ghat, abusing them.

5

Sitting in his chamber, Geshe Jampa's fingers reached the call bell. He pushed it slowly and keeping his both hands behind his head, he took support of the back of the chair. Shaking his chair to and fro slowly. He was feeling unrest. The air-conditioner, mat on the floor, curtains, chairs, everything in the room seemed to be suffocating him.

'Yes Gela?'

A peon of the institute stood before him.

'Switch off the A.C. and open the windows.'

'Yes Gela.'

And the peon hastily had opened all the windows of room.

'See, don't send anyone to meet me now. Only Devyani madam will come after taking her period. You inform me.'

'Jee, what I'll say to her?' He was confused a little bit.

'Oh, I have called her for some necessary assignments, so let her come. Other visitors may meet me afterward. You tell them.'

'Yes Gela.'

The peon went out.

Geshe Jampa had a glance at the Ashok Stambh[1] on the Sarnath lawn through the window. A symbol of compassion emerged from big human annihilation. A monument of peace. Standing with pride for many years. Will one more Ashoka take birth again who can repent on the human annihilation of today? Will he also make a stupa of remembrance out of compassion produced into his heart? The monument of peace and co-existence?

---

1. Ashok Stambh-A huge pillar in Sarnath made by emperor Ashoka in memory of Lord Buddha.

His mind was roaming in the streets of peace and unrest and slowly it reached his motherland.

Mag-pa came to his house at Nang-gar-che[1] in the darkness of night. Someone knocked at the door slowly and father asked—

'Who is there?'

Father's voice was frightened because there was a rumour spreading all over in Lhasa[2] from two days. A crowd of millions of people had surrounded Norbulinkha[3] coming out from Lhasa city, so that Chinese can not arrest His Holiness the Dalai Lama. The skirmish had taken place twice between Khampa-guerilla and Chinese soldiers. Tibetan public is in strong anger. Situation may be explosive anytime. Perhaps it is for the first time in peace loving Tibet that the public is opposing so strongly the exploitation by China.

Father used to listen to the news on the radio all the time. The news broadcast of B.B.C. and voice of America were increasing the heart-beating of Tibetans. The people of remote areas in Tibet were frightened of something unusual happening.

The village Nang-gar-che was more cold than other villages of Tibet even in the month of March also, when the weather of whole Tibet was very pleasant. Perhaps the reason was that it was situated fourteen-fifteen thousand feet higher from sea-level. Everybody was confined to his house in Nang-gar-che.

'Please open the door. It is Chhering'. Mag-pa's slow voice came from outside the door.

Little Jampa sprang out of happiness— 'Mama, Mag-pa has come.' He ran away inside the house to inform his mother.

'Why are you shouting Jampa? Speak slowly son.' Instructing him, Mama came out from the kitchen.

She put the lamp near the threshold of the kitchen so that light may spread both sides. Hearing the creaking sound of the opening door, the flock of sheeps sitting in the porch became attentive.

---

1. Name of a place in Tibet.
2. Name of famous place in Tibet.
3. Name of place in Tibet related to His Holiness the Dalai Lama.

Father assured them with his typical sound of 'Hui-Hui' and they sat in their place again and started chewing cud. When the smell of their urine came in with the gust of air then it was known that a speedy wind was also blowing outside with cold.

Taking Mag-pa inside the room father latched the door again. Coming inside the room, groaning Mag-pa fell down on the bed laying on his belly.

'What happened Mag-pa?' Mama was puzzled.

'Oh….water….water.' Mag-pa was groaning.

'How….these wounds?'

Father cried almost. It was bleeding from the back of Mag-pa. The cloth was torn. A big hole was clearly visible from which blood was coming out. Little Jampa also watched.

'Father, anyhow I could come here escaping myself. Many people were killed there.' Mag-pa tried to explain. Mama had brought water in meanwhile.

'Don't give water Jampa's mama. Bring tea mixed with butter. Mag-pa is wounded. Treatment should be done.'

Telling it, father went out almost running towards the valley in front of house. Perhaps he had gone to bring some medicinal plant. Jampa was watching Mag-pa with surprise.

Cleansing the wound of Mag-pa, father had applied the medicinal paste. The tea mixed with butter made Mag-pa somehow conscious. Father asked him—

'Where did this battle take place?'

'At Norbulinkha. There were many people of Tibetan organizations and Khampa guerillas in security of His Holiness the Dalai Lama. Millions of people were there.'

The past scenario again became live before the eyes of Mag-pa.

'Then?' Father was asking in perplexity.

'They started bombarding Norbulinkha and after that they diverted the direction of cannons towards the city. They did not leave the Potala temple and the monasteries around it.'

'O God, a huge genocide. So many Tibetan people will be assassinated.'

'Yes, we could not know that how many people were killed in Lhasa City but inside and outside the Norbulinkha more than a thousand were shot dead.'

Mag-pa was not afraid but restless.

'Is His Holiness…?' Father could not complete his sentence.

'No, he is safe. He was brought out to a safe place two days before.'

Mag-pa's voice was confident.

'The buildings of Norbulinkha are safe or not?'

'No, many buildings inside had been ruined. But it is surprising that the temple of Mahakaal is completely secured in between. I was near that very temple that is why could I get saved.'

'Where is my Kon-Chog?' Mama was upset.

'Yes, yes, where is Kon-chog?'

Now father also remembered. Cho-cho[1] Kon-chog had gone with Mag-pa one week before. They had not told their whereabouts.

'Perhaps he must be safe completely. He had already reached Keshung[2] village with Khampa-fighters.'

Mag-pa was unveiling the secret slowly.

'Why…why Keshung?'

'There he is also in security of His Holiness the Dalai Lama.'

'But when did he become a Khampa-fighter?'

There was a lost freshness of countenance on her face.

'Long ago mama.'

'Why did you not tell? Why, tell me.'

Mama shook Mag-pa's hand out of frustration. The heart of a mother was worried for her son.

'We were waiting for a proper time. Now that has come.'

Mag-pa was gazing at the smoky roof of the room.

'Is he safe? How far will his journey with them be?'

---

1. Cho cho- Address to elder brother.
2. Keshung- A village in Tibet.

'The answers of both questions are uncertain at present.'

Told Mag-pa looking at mama intensely.

'Will they go by leaving Tibet?'

Now father was asking.

'There are dangers now here. This step was necessary for public welfare and as well as for the country also.'

Little Jampa had never seen this part of Mag-pa's personality. At present he was not laughing and story-telling Mag-pa. He seemed something different from previous days.

'How many people are with…?'

Mama was depressed.

'Many people are with him.'

'will all leave their own Tibet?'

The question of mama was full of agony and confusion.

'No, some of them will go out and co-operate us from there. We won't allow any country to make Tibet its colony. Our people will give support from outside in this mission. We shall continue our freedom movement inside the country.'

'O God, Chinaye was lost. My lap had become barren already. Now Kon-Chog also….?'

Mama was weeping bitterly. The house walls seemed to tremble with her sobbing. Frightened Jampa went near to Mama and sat in her lap. He was also loosing his patience.

'Mama, what happened with Cho-cho Kon-chog? Mama tell me… speak something…mama?'

Wiping her tears with his fingers Jampa wept bitterly.

'Please, don't weep Jampa's mama. It is not time to weep. Anytime guarding police may come outside the door.'

Father tried to console her.

Jampa also had watched the several riders in soldiers' dress around Nang-gar-che in these ten to fifteen days. On that day also, sheep were grazing in the green grass field of Yum-Dog-Chho,[1] and

---

1. Yum-Dog-Chho- A very large pond of Tibet that has become almost dry but there is water place to place.

Jampa was playing with his friend on a high rock. From there he could watch his sheep and field also which was situated behind a small hill. The large circumference of Yum-Dog-Chho was visible and spread before him. A thin current of water seemed to assemble in this huge pond here and there. The water of this pond was very sweet in taste. The chain of small and big hills in the mid of this pond, seemed as if a river was surrounding this hilly area.

'I am emperor. You bring water for me.' Sitting on a higher rock, little Jampa ordered his friend. The game of king and minister was going on. Sheep were grazing in the field freely.

'Yes me Lord.'

As his friend turned to bring water, Jampa murmured from behind—

'Hush, look there. Soldiers on horses. Let us hide ourselves.'

And they both hid themselves behind the big rock. Four riders came out from the hill side. Jampa could not differentiate whether they were Chinese or Tibetan soldiers. Merely he had heard the rumours of soldiers roaming here and there and it created a kind of fear in him. The sound of foot-steps of horses reached them. The sheep bleated for a moment and then engaged in grazing. When the sound of horse-steps went far away, they peeped from behind the rock. The soldiers were disappearing behind the hills.He forgot the game of King and minister. Hastily he drove away the sheep and reached home. When he told the whole incident to his mama, she clung to him with her chest. She could not utter anything.

When Cho cho Kon-Chog and Mag-pa returned home, Jampa told them about the soldiers he had seen—

'Cho-cho Kon-Chog, they had worn the brown coats and cap of artificial hairs.'

'Why didn't you hit them with a stone?'

A deep disgust for them was in the voice of Cho-cho Kon-chog.

'Why Kon-Chog… what are you teaching Jampa? Is this our religion?'

Mama burst out on Cho-cho Kon-Chog.

'You don't understand mama! Gradually they are increasing their number in our city. Now a days they are encroaching the villages of Tibet also. Land requisition is being done without proper cost and roads are being made in the names of development. The fertile lands of farmers are being gulped up. The farmers are working hard with them as labourers and being exploited also for remuneration. Above these, they say that we feel pride that Tibet is returning to its motherland.

The face of Cho-cho Kon-Chog was red with anger.

Mama was listening to everything carefully supporting her chin on her palm. The yellow scarf was hanging downward on her head and Jampa was playing with it.

'Do you know mother-in-law that why Tibet is suffering from inflation? Why the cost of grains have increased ten times and butter nine times?'

When Mag-pa told mama, she became curious.

'Why Mag-pa? I don't know'. She asked.

'They have taken two thousand ton barley as the meal of millions of their soldiers from our country. They have encroached a large area of our country for their camp. That is why, wherever they go in Tibet, the people throw stones at them. The people shout slogans of protest. At this time they have come in the name of development in Tibet but it is suspected that they will make it their colony later on.'

How this worry of Mag-pa that day has taken its shape, Jampa was live-evidence of it.

'Our Government is also a culprit. Why is it allowing them to come?'

Mama was aggressive.

'We were deceived mother-in-law. The signature was taken on an agreement keeping us in dark that some feudalist forces have entered China and Tibet both and to drive them away the liberation-fighters of China are permitted to enter Tibet. Also in one clause of the agreement, it has been mentioned that Tibetan people co-operating with Chinese Liberation-fighters will drive away these feudalist forces from Tibet and will merge into its larger family, that is China, while history tells that there was no foreign-rule in Tibet since after 1912.

Mag-pa was explaining the political situation and brother Kon-chog was listening to it very seriously.

'There are so many attractive clauses and promises also in that agreement, as development of farming, political situation and rules, not to pressurize them to improve the life-standard of Tibetan people protecting their religion, culture and faiths, not to change their political situation and rules, not to pressurize them to accept these reformations, etc. On that basis they got the chance to enter our land. But most dangerous clauses are those, through which they have exploited us, to devoid Tibet from all rights of foreign-policy and merging of Tibetan soldiers with Chinese Forces. This very point is a big danger for our existence and is also the evidence of their evil intention. We all have to protest against it.'

'But it is very hard to face them Mag-pa. It is not an easy task.'

'We must be organized Mama. If we shall not sacrifice at present, our coming generation will not excuse us.'

'But how Mag-pa?'

Mama was worried till now. Jampa was also being worried watching others. The whole matter, being mysterious and difficult for him but was indicating its destiny. Mag-pa told further— 'India is our teacher-country mother-in-law. See, how the Indian people, by organizing themselves, had thrown away the British-ruler from their country. Why do not we?'

'They had world-support with them. They raised their voices by going to many countries. But we are aloof from the very beginning. We did not join even UNO, nor maintain any political relation with other countries. We ourselves are faulty for this situation Mag-pa.'

Cho cho Kon-chog was in deep agony.

'No need to be depressed but it is time to awake and make others awakened. We must try to bring our people back who are supporting them entrapped in their allurement and attractive but false promises.

And after that day, Cho cho Kon-chog and Mag-pa went out once, then only wounded Mag-pa returned. Mama and father was shocked hearing the news that Kon-Chog had joined the guerilla organization and the recent news about Norbulinkha.

'Thak….Thak….thak…' A loud tapping sound at the door shook all of them. Mama's sobbings were stopped due to fear. She gave a silent hint to Mag-pa to go out from the backdoor and herself reached the small window of the room—

'Who is there?' She asked making her voice slightly harsh. Jampa had watched Mag-pa who was going out from the back door with his staggering legs hastily. Father moved ahead quickly and shut the back door after Mag-pa.

'Open the door. We have to check the house.' A rough and growling voice came from outside.

'What for?' Mama had filled a touch of surprise in her voice knowingly.

'Open first, then I tell.'

The door was tapped loudly by the kick of shoes. Mama looked towards father out of fear. The confusion 'what should be done' was reflecting in her eyes. Father indicated her to stay a while and himself opened the door latch. The door was pushed with stroke from outside as father had opened it and dashed together on his face. Father lurched on one side. A painful cry came out of his throat and he sat on the floor holding his face in both of his hands.

'Oh, what happened Jampa's father?' Mama supported him at once and caught him in her arms.

'Beat this stupid man.' A policeman ordered his companions. Three-four policemen had entered the room at that time. Ordered by senior police officer, one of them stretched his gun towards father. Shocked Jampa cried and adhered with the legs of policemen. He requested—

'Please don't kill my Pala[1] .... please be kind to us.'

The tears were flowing from his eyes.

Meanwhile Mama hastily caught the barrel of gun stretched on the chest of father and diverted its direction forcibly towards roof. The trigger of the gun was pushed by the policemen and bullet passed up piercing the roof of clay and hay. A kind of wrestling began between Mama and that policeman. Mama was pushing him out the door and he wanted to capture father striking Mama on one side. The another policeman kicked Jampa away clinging with his leg and brought out his hunter. He hit on Mama's waist by his hunter. She writhed out of pain. When father saw this situation, he was out of self in anger. He caught the policeman by the neck who hit mama with the hunter and pushed his head on wall twice thrice. Hearing his loud cry the other policeman saw behind and attacked father. They started beating father by their shoes and butt of gun and reacting also—

'You are becoming leader? Now, call your companions to come and save you. Call your His Holiness to show his wonder.'

'Why are you beating so cruelly. What is our crime?'

Weeping bitterly Mama covered father laying on his body. The hunters were striking her for some time. Jampa was watching this cruel scene standing in a corner of the room and weeping loudly. A policeman stopped everyone and told—

'Stay a while. First of all ask these people that someone had been hidden here or not?'

'Yes, yes, tell.... had someone come this side to hide himself.'

The another policeman growled stopping his hunter.

'No ....'. Mama's weak voice came out to protect Mag-pa.

'She will not reveal the truth in this way. Catch her son.'

One policeman caught Jampa by his shoulders. Little Jampa cried out of fear-

'Mama, save me ....'

'Please leave him. I tell... I tell you.'

---

1. Pala-Father.

Mama was almost confused.

'He ran away from the back-door.'

Mama indicated towards the door. Her face was wet with tears.

'Now you are telling when you made him to run away. Hold her child, and bring with us.'

The policeman, who had held Jampa, pushed him towards the door.

'No, please don't capture me. I'll not go leaving my Mama.'

He cried.

'Keep quite…..' A stroke of hunter fell down on his back too. He wept bitterly out of pain.

'Who was that fellow? Where did he run away? What was your relation?'

One was asking Mama.

'My son-in-law.' Mama was telling.

'What was his name?'

'Chhering.'

'Give his address otherwise we are bringing your son with us. You will come to know when we'll make him guerilla against you people. If you can't understand our simple language, we know the technique to make you understand by other means.'

The second one was gazing at father with angry eyes.

'Please trust me sir. I'll handover him to you very soon as he is found.'

Father requested them with folded hands.

'Well done…. Where will you search us to hand-over him.'

The policeman laughed ironically.

'Please, have faith in my words sir. He was not a criminal sir. I don't know why he went out hearing your tapping on the door. Perhaps he was frightened. Sir, so many news are being heard now a days. May be…'

Father presented a new pretension to protect Mag-pa.

'We are thinking about your welfare and reformation and you people oppose us?'

'Oh no sir. Why we'll oppose? We are very happy to know your policy sir.'

Jampa was understanding well that father was trying to subside the situation at present.

'Leave his child. We shall come back again after one week. Any how we must get the whereabouts of your Mag-pa, otherwise the result you might be knowing. Why not we believe that he is also involved in this agitation.'

They all went. Mama and father did not get any news about Mag-pa and hence they decided at once to send Jampa to India with other children of the village across the border of Tibet.

'But Mama, with whom I'll live there?'

When little Jampa came to know their decision, he asked in perplexity. In the night Mama had prepared the packets of Masung and Jyupa for the journey. She was continuously weeping. In every preparation, she was being emotional and her tears broke the limits. After the separation from Chinaye and Kon-Chog, now the departure of little Jampa was very intolerable for her. Her eyes were red due to tears. Father was watching Jampa and Mama one after another and was helpless to do anything. He became silent. Very often he used to call Jampa and taking him into his lap he kissed his forehead and murmured-

'Oum Manipadme Hum .... O God! Save my child.'

'I'll not go Pala.'

Little Jampa was puzzled to see his parents' condition.

'No my son, we can't make you stay here. If you will go there, your life is safe but if they will take you with them, what will happen? Only God knows.'

Father's eyes were dry like stones. 'If Mag-pa will come back, they will not bring me back?'

Jampa was also afraid.

'Nothing can be said my son. Nothing. Neither we are assured about Mag-pa's coming back nor we can think of their mentality. It is being heard that forcibly they take Tibetan children and train them to hold guns against their own culture and country. Sometimes, there is bad news also about these children.'

Not mentioning the horrible situation before him, father was silent but he trembled to think its horrible output.

After a long time, Jampa could know the fact that the Tibetan children are being converted into communists, forcibly snatching them from their parents. If they protest, they were arrested or shot dead. Chinese officers used to give logic behind it that parents could work better without their children, so these children were sent to Chinese centres in order to get proper education. Jampa also heard that Lamas were tortured specially. The allegation on them was that they are dependent on other's money without any labour. So, facing cruel behaviour, these Lamas were being sent to work-centres. Specially the old aged Lamas were so tortured that they liked to opt death.

At last, that moment came when Jampa left his mama's finger for ever. Pushing one edge of her shawl in her mouth, she was trying to stop her sobbings but could not succeed. Tears were constantly flowing from her eyes and she was posing herself busy in keeping the luggage of Jampa. After loading all the goods on the back of a mule, when father caught Jampa's hand from his mother, the heart of little Jampa seemed to be crushed. It seemed that something was creating hindrance in his throat. Getting helpless, he clung to the waist of his mother.

'Mama, I can't go. Please, don't send me.' He wept bitterly. Mama's patience was also broken. She embraced Jampa and requested his father—

'For God sake, please you and I also should go with Jampa. How will my child live there alone? How will he reach across the mountain?' there was beseeching in her voice.

Father's voice also became wet. He said—

Jampa's mother, am I cruel to my son? How we can go with him leaving our house here, fields, sheep. Had you not heard of Dorje? He was going across the Tibetan border carrying his children and was captured very much here, this side of the mountain, and imprisoned. His children were caught away somewhere else. If there are only children, no one suspects, otherwise I could not send my Jampa alone.

Father convinced her. Jampa was clinging yet to his Mama's chest. With the warmth of mother's affection, her heart beating was also echoing in his ears that he could remember till today. Since then, Jampa could never embrace his mother, nor could hear those affectionate heart-beats.

In deep frustration Mama made Jampa to depart from her and gave instructions to him—

'See, be careful in climbing the hills. Whenever you feel excessive cold, cover yourself with Chuk-tu also.

Jampa saw her with sorrowful eyes and shook his head in acceptance.

'Sleep in the midst of children at night. Take someone with you while going to the toilet at night.'

"Hmm…". Jampa's weeping burst out. This was his weak point. He could not go alone at night, even for toilet. Mama or father used to go with him.

'Don't be nervous Jampa! There is proper arrangement for you across the border. You will not be an orphan there. There is proper arrangement of education and accommodation for the Tibetan refugees with the cooperation of the Government of India. These refugee children are being looked after very carefully there.'

Father was trying to console both of them by explaining the arrangements for refugees in India whatever he had heard from others in these days.

'Will you go with Jampa up to the border?'

She was asking being impatient.

'I will try my best to return when they climb the hills and cross our border, then there will no danger, for them. But God may know further.

He caught the finger of Jampa.

'Always try to send your whereabouts son.'

Mama's pathetic weeping began to break the deep silence of the valley of yum-Dog-chho.

"Oh, Mama….."

Memories of Mama were again knocking the door of his heart in Sarnath.

Geshe Jampa stood from his chair out of deep agony. He could hear the sobbing of his Mama in his chamber till now. He came into the present. Since then till today neither he could get any information about his Mama nor be able to send his whereabouts to her. God knows, in which condition Mama and father will be living there?

Perhaps Mama would have been so old that hardly one can recognize her face, but her affectionate warmth and heart-beating will be her ever introduction. Perhaps Mama too hardly can recognize her Jampa now. Little Jampa himself will be in her memory. How many things have been changed during these thirty to thirty five years. He had completed his education in this very monastery and with the honour of Geshe he was selected as head of this institution to teach Tibetan children and inspire them to know themselves and live with their roots. Alas, if Mama could also have been here.

Geshe Jampa began walking in his chamber out of restlessness. Ashoka's pillar in the form of a monument was clearly visible through his window. He watched the clock. He remembered, it will be the last period of Devyani. She will be coming in a few moments. How cognitive she looks in her talk. She is well aware of her surroundings also, as well as about her subject of teaching. She watches everything with her penetrating eyes and gives her fearless comments on it, without caring that someone may take it otherwise.

'Sir, do you not think that in scientific society of today, when you people are engaged in your non-violent freedom movement, there is the need of brave soldiers, not of monks?'

Only a few days before she asked Geshe Jampa talking on the issue of religion.

'What do you mean Devyani?' His voice was calm and quite.

'My intention is to let you know that a few months ago, here, in Sarnath one hundred and sixty two Tibetans became monks. There is restriction on the modern education of Tibetans in Tibet on the one side and on the other side they are holding tightly to the same old customs here in India. Do you think that you people will get freedom through these monks?'

'Devyani, will you listen to me for a minute.' He told her with a smile.

'Yes sir, please, tell.'

She looked at him but thoughts were coming and going into her mind.

'You might be knowing the saint of Sabarmati. He is our ideal. He fought against British rule through non-violence, and did not adopt violence.'

'But Gela, excuse me, I cannot agree with your statement. What do you think that we Indians got freedom only through non-violence? Was there no any contribution of revolutionaries like Chandrashekhar Aazad, Bhagat Singh, Lala Lajpat Rai or Subhash Chandra Bose etc? The Zeal to cut down ones own head for the cause of the Motherland was flowing in the blood of almost every young Indian. Aggressive and non-aggressive currents, both were running side by side at that time. There was pressure from all sides on the Britishers then we could get our freedom,'

Devyani was explaining with pride without caring his happiness or unhappiness. Geshe Jampa was answerless for few moments.

'Actually Devyani, His Holiness the Dalai Lama cannot support any kind of violence. He believes that the accomplishment of truth cannot be achieved through violence. If the means are not right, how can its result be? So we observe the liberation of Tibet in the context of world peace and human-welfare.'

While speaking he was looking at the wall in front of him. Devyani was observing his face seriously. The other teachers were also in his chamber at that time and listening to him.

'Then what do you think that your Tibet will be liberated through these policies, living in another country?'

Devyani raised her next question.

Whispering in her ear Balendu Thapaliyal, who sat beside her, forbade her to argue so much.

'No, No, Thapaliyal, don't hesitate. The discussions on this topic must be open. It is not a matter to hide. Such type of questions that how we can get freedom of Tibet living in other countries, are very often rising in the minds of Indians. For freedom we have to come down in the field. For this purpose we are trying our best and making efforts also. Gradually we are sending there the group of Tibetan people who believe in non-violence. Now, really it looks hard to run our freedom-movement by living abroad.'

Geshe Jampa's voice was calm and cool.

Devyani filled with guilt suddenly.

'Gela, excuse me please. I did not mean that you people are a burden for we Indians… I mean… we think that you are burdensome…'. She was confused what to say.

'Need not to be sorry Devyani. I know your emotions. India is also co-operating as much as possible. It has its own policies with China. We don't expect anything beyond our limit. We also want that relation between China and India should be normal. But for this reason also it is necessary that a peace-loving country like Tibet must play its role of buffer-state as usual otherwise there may be problems between two big powerful countries.'

Devyani did not give any logic further. Only, she looked constantly at his face for sometime. Balendu Thapaliyal had gone to take his period, seeking permission from him. Gradually his chamber vacated one by one, only Devyani was still sitting with reflection of pros and cons. He himself asked—

'Is there no period today Devyani?'

'Yes, it is sir… Sir, you have taken my argument otherwise?'

She was puzzled.

He smiled at her clear heartedness.

'No, why should I feel otherwise? What wrong have you told?'

'Actually, I feel that I should not say all these things.'

'Why? Only for this reason that I am head of this institution? For this only agreeable-untruth must be spoken?'

He laughed.

'But harsh-truth is also forbidden sir by our sages. '*Ma Bruyat Satyamapriyam.*[1]'

She also laughed slowly. A life floating into her eyes, he saw that day.

'Stay for a while. Have a cup of tea and then move from here.'

He pushed the call-bell. She felt uneasy. Perhaps this was for the first time, when she was alone in his chamber, otherwise most of the time she was with the other employees of the institution in some important meetings or discussions. He could feel her uncomfort, and in keeping himself neutral, he started to read a magazine picking it up from his table.

Devyani's eyes were also wandering here and there in the chamber. Tibetan pieces of art of handicrafts and paintings on the wall were as usual as in previous days but today Devyani silently started to invent new meanings in it. Her eyes stayed on a picture. In the centre of a rectangular flag there was an enlightened sun from which six red and six blue rays were coming out. She had found a medium to lessen the heaviness of the atmosphere.

'Sir, these blue and red rays of sun are symbol of what?'

'Your question is oblique.'

He laughed. Closing the magazine he further stated—

'This is a symbol of the Tibetan race. The yellow border of three sides of the flag is the symbol of Bauddh religion.'

'It means Bauddh religion itself is the national religion of Tibet?'

---

1. A verse of Sanskrit language meaning harsh truth should not be spoken.

Devyani had got the chance to continue the dialogue.

'Obiously, it is very clear. As there are Islamic countries, Hindu nations, in the same way Tibet had also its own religion. Because India is the origin of this religion, so we Tibetans admit it as our Guru Desh, the teacher country. Thus you are also my teacher, my Guru, my mentor.'

He laughed loudly. His calm and cool face glittered with the simplicity of an innocent child.

'Oh Gela, you….please?

Devyani felt shy. She could not reply to him and again diverted her dialogue to the flag.

'Well, this glittering stone between two lions and white triangle in this flag will be certainly the symbol of something?'

'Yes Devayani! This white triangle is symbolic of icy mountains and you know that Tibet is an icy-land. Now, this glittering stone and light is defined by me in some other way.

As the Tibetans are religious minded by habit and a worshipper of nature too hence they have never disturbed the equilibrium of nature. They have never exploited the gemmiferous earth, as other nations do. This was the reason the environment of Tibet was very rich and pollution-free. But now a days China is misusing it. To make atom-bombs, its experiments…. and then the wastage of it is being-thrown in the rivers. There is plenty of gold, silver and crome in the area of Ado-Zod,[1] Chhusumzod of Tibet[2].'

He became serious again remembering the miseries of his country.

'Gela, this flag is the national emblem of your exiled government?'

Devyani's voice was very soft. She had observed his agony for his nation.

"Hmm…". Supporting his face in both of his palms, he put his elbows on the table and sat silently.

---

1. Name of place in Tibet.
2. Name of place in Tibet.

After having a cup of tea, seeking permission Devyani had gone from his chamber but made him restless. His mind reached his motherland and wandered in the green but dejected valleys of Tibet.

There were two villages named Chhu-shor-gy-pon and Lha-Dong at few distance from Gyanchi when they crossed Kharu-la. Jampa was climbing Kharu-La holding his father's finger. The mule with luggage on its back was moving ahead. When Jampa was tired, father used to make him sit on the bundle of luggage on the back of mule. He himself was walking on foot behind the mule. The clay was black here before Kharu-La so the colour of water of the river also looked black. There was ice and snow here and there on the peaks of mountains. The small rocks were laying in the way. Green grass was visible in the large field where wild deer and sheep were grazing. The faces of shepherds were full of fear and curiousity both. In the valley of mountain, the small green plants of Dhoop were seen.

'Making these plants dry and mixing perfume in it, the people of this area make scented sticks for worship. This is their main profession.'

Father had engaged him in discourse. Sometimes he used to look here and there with suspicious eyes.

'Will the children of these houses also go from here?'

Jampa's question hurt his father. He rubbed softly Jampa's head out of grief and said—

'No son, how can all go? And you are going there for a better life. Why you become nervous? When you will become worthy, we shall call you back my son.'

'Then why are you not coming with me?' he insisted again.

'How will Mama live alone in the house? Hun ...'

Father tried to divert him by a weak logic.

'Then let us go back. Bring Mama also. We have passed a small distance only.'

He again insisted. He felt as if someone was squeezing his heart.

'No Jampa. We have come far from Nang-gar-che. So large Yum-dog-chho has been crossed by us. Miles of fields, then after climbing of Kharu-La and now we are about to reach Gyanchi. Oh no son. I don't have courage now to go back.'

Anyhow father had convinced him.

'If in our absence, those policemen will come? What will Mama do? They will again beat mama. They will bring her with them.'

Jampa was again about to weep.

Father gave a solution.

'If they break the door? Then…?'

Frightened Jampa's next question sprang towards his father.

'No, they will not come so soon. Also I have instructed your Mama to go to Eshin's house to sleep at night on the other hill.'

'But if they go to Eshin aunt's house also, then?'

Uttering this, Jampa again began to sob for Mama.

'See Jampa, don't weep! Otherwise some lion or bear will come out from these caves.'

Father told indicating towards naturally made caves in the hills.

'See Jampa, now we shall cross this river by Kwa.'[1]

Father applied another idea to make him diverted. He was successful. Jampa became happy.

'But how this mule will come?'

Again Jampa was puzzled.

'This mule?... Oh…. I shall drive it forward through that way.'

Father indicated towards a hill at distance.

'But who will show the path to mule?

'I shall show.'

'Then, shall I be alone in Kwa?'

Jampa again frightened.

'Yes. We shall both meet on that side of the river.'

'No I'll not sit in Kwa. I'll be with you.'

He caught father in his arms.

---

1. Kwa-A boat made of leather.

'Do you know Jampa, in winter season this river freezes and people cross it on foot itself. Then, there is no need to go to that hillside.'

Turning towards that path father was describing.

After some moments, when they were climbing the hill, a tornado came and made them to sit in a natural cave. The mule was standing outside the cave and father hid Jampa in his shawl. A gust of rain also came in a few moments. It was rare weather for the spring season. The rain drops pounded on the green tips of grass after the gust had gone. The golden sun-ball was reflecting in those water drops from the back of the hills. The drops were drizzling by the stroke of steps.

Jampa forgot everything for sometime observing this beauty of nature. There appeared a rainbow across that very river. It was an enchanting beauty of nature. The hills were standing like pillars on both edges and a colourful rainbow was making an arch on it. The greenery was spread-out in the valley. The fields of mustard also were seen across the river here and there. The yellow flowers of mustard were swaying with the wind. The small cottages of shepherds and Dokpa-community looked like a painting. The smoke raising from the cottages indicated that a meal was being cooked. They were moving ahead watching the beauty of nature. Some farmers were ploughing their fields also.

'Let us have tea.' Father proposed watching his tired face.

'Yes.' Jampa rubbed his lips with his tongue. Really he was tired, thirsty and hungry too.

They stopped in a shop after some distance. There, they took their meal of parched grain and butter-mixed tea in a wooden-cup and again started their journey. They had to reach the next village before evening and join some other companions there, they had to proceed towards the border of India. Chhu-shor-gy-pon village was just before the village Lha-Dong. There were many ruins of ancient buildings in this valley. Jampa asked out of curiosity—

'Who lives in it?'

'Not living but lived.'

Father told him stopping his mule in front of a small house. Two children from this house also had to go with Jampa.

'Where have they gone? Have they also left their village?'

Jampa was sad seeing those ruins. At the same time an old lady came out from that house. Her face was filled with deep wrinkles. A heavy silver-necklace and big nose-pin in her nose had become dull with the passage of time. The Pangchhen, symbol of her marriage was hanging over Chhupa and she wore a woollen sleeveless jacket over her long blouse. A scarf of red colour was also hanging from her head on her back in the same style as his Mama. Jampa was again reminded of his mother.

'Oh, you have come Thupthen? Come, come inside.'

She addressed father by his name and told in whispering voice.

'Yes Aachaa¹. Here is Jampa are the children are ready?'

Father was asking moving inside the house. The mule was tied to a small tree outside the house and green grass was in front of it.

'Yes, all are ready. Only you try to make their father understand. He is also insisting to go to India. He says, who will live here to die? Now, you also think over, should we all vacate Tibet and hand it over to them? Is this a proper way to think? If one has to die, he can die wherever he will be. If we shall die in Tibet, at least our body of clay will merge into the clay of Tibet.'

The old lady was opening the door of inner room and murmuring also.

'Aachaa, is there any news from the village Lha-Dong or not?'

'They all are also ready. This time you take rest here. Move in the morning. Journey at night is dangerous. It will take only one hour in reaching Lha-Dong through this descending of the hill on the right side.'

She was groping in the darkness to kindle the lamp. Jampa saw a man sitting in a corner bent-headed in the dim light of lamp. The

---

1. Aachaa-Elder sister.

man was wearing a cap of artificial hairs on his head. The leather-shoes were put beside on the floor.

'Chheeu! Cheeu!'

Father called him up and he raised his head. Perhaps it was his nick-name.

'What is matter Cheeu?'

'Cho cho[1], you see. Mama doesn't let me go. I don't want to live here.'

He was about to weep. Jampa was surprised that how elderly Cheeu uncle wants to go leaving his mother alone here.

'You gabble as much as you wish, but you have not to go. Is Thupten also going leaving his country?'

The old lady, moving towards kitchen, told. Jampa thought that his Mama also would have retained him from going there in the same manner.

'What will you eat Jampa? Rice and Chamari[2] meat or something else?'

The old lady was asking.

Father told before Jampa uttered anything.

'Nothing Aachaa. Just before few minutes we have taken Jyupa and tea. Only we want to sleep now so that the further journey may be easy.'

'How do you talk Thupten? Will this child survive without meat in these frozen hills? This time he must take Thuk-pa[3] and tomorrow I shall pack some dry meat for his journey. Move early in the morning. Why Jampa, perhaps you are not afraid of going, isn't it?'

Jampa was constantly surprised watching her fearlessness and patience. Contrary to it, Mama was weeping bitterly when he was parting form her. How fearless is this old lady?

'May I come in sir?'

1.　Cho- cho- Elder brother.
2.　Chamari-An wild animal like deer.
3.　Thuk-pa-Soup.

The voice of Devyani at present had broken the chain of memories of various incidents of Geshe Jampa's past. He came back to the present and saw behind him. Devyani was standing there.

'Oh sir, have I disturbed you? You were contemplating something.'

Devyani was asking with guilt when she saw him standing in front of the window and in a thoughtful mood.

'No, No. Devayani. Come in. I was waiting for you.'

Suddenly he was ashamed slightly at his sentence. Correcting it, he again told—

'I mean, I had called you for some urgent matter.'

'Yes sir, please tell.'

A sweet smile was floating on her lips. Eyes were slightly bent-down out of shyness.

'Some children have come from Dharmshala. Tibetan refugees don't know anything except their own language. You teach them Hindi so that they can adjust here.'

To remove his hesitation, Geshe Jampa at once put his proposal before her. He did not ask her to sit even.

'Yes sir. Then should I….?'

She wanted to ask to go.

'You kindly meet Maai Dolma. The rest I'll make clear to you tomorrow. Take an introduction with the children.'

His sentences were scattered.

'Yes sir, should I go?'

She was asking. Today her hair was not open. Wrapping it a tuft was made behind and a jasmine flower was cobbled on it. The flower was visible from her earside.

'Oh, yes…if you don't want to sit… you may go.'

Geshe Jampa's own answer seemed unnatural and confused.

'Jee, Tashi Delek sir.'

She stayed for a while and turned suddenly to go.

6

Listening to the tapping sound on the main gate of her house, Devyani peeped from the window of her room. Who may it be? Nobody comes to meet her this late at night, she thought.

'Who is there?' Lobjang asked from her room.

'It is I, Tanchu Dhondhap. Please open the door.'

The visitor introduced himself. The bulb of the porch switched on and a light spread out as his introductory sentence finished. The switch of the bulb was inside Lobang's room. Shutting down her window Devyani saw the face of the visitor in the light. The thin nose and small eyes in the same manner on his healthy body was his introduction. She could not understand as why faces of all Tibetans looked like same. Same fair complexion, thin lips, small eyes as if coming out from the skin of cheeks. Only changes in dresses were often seen. Someone in monks' dress, someone in modern dress like jeans or loose shirts. This visitor also wore a white shirt on black jeans.

'Oye, Dhondhap, how have you come so late at night?' Opening the latch of the main gate, Lobjang was asking with surprise.

'Oh, as usual Mama. There was a meeting of the Tibetan youth Congress here in Sarnath. I thought, why should I stay in a guest house?'

He entered. Devyani had seen him through the window hole.

'Well done son! Why has Seering not come with you?'

Lobjang was asking closing the gate behind.

'It was not proper to come with her in the meeting.'

He laughed lifting his shoulders and moved inside.

'Who is Didi?'[1]

---

1. Didi- Address to elder sister in Hindi.

Younger brother Deepesh stood beside his sister Devyani.

'The same person, about whom Lobjang was telling that day that is her step son-in-law... Tanchu Dhondhap'

Devyani closed the window completely.

'Well, well. Makhanchu has come?'

Making fun of him Deepesh laughed.

'Oh Deepesh, you are studying in M.A. When you will become civilized? You are speaking so loudly. If he hears to you then what?'

Devyani was slightly angry at him.

'Who came Devyani?'

Devyani's mother also came from the next room.

'No one Mama. No one has come to our house. A guest has come to our landlord.'

Devyani assured her mother.

'Mama, guest of Lobjang aunt has come, Makhanchu Dhondhapji.'

Deepesh shook his mother's shoulders slowly, whispering in her ear. Devyani could not help but to laugh. She spoke with superficial anger—

'Look Mama, tomorrow our landlord will tell us to pack-up our luggage from this house. Tanchu Dhondhap is her son-in-law, editor of Daser magazine and this Deepesh...'

Devyani's sentence remained incomplete because Lobjang had appeared there opening the door. A glimpse of hurry and shyness was blended on her face.

'O Madam, a request....'

'Yes Lobjangji, please tell me.'

Devyani spoke pushing away her chair towards her. She was doubtful that Lobjang has listened to Deepesh, but when Lobjang made a request, her doubt was removed.

'O Madaam, actually... there is no milk in my kitchen. Milk is essential for Lamaji before he goes to sleep, so I gave him. Who knew that someone will come at this time. My daughter's husband has come. If you can provide me for tea... Pema has also not come yet otherwise I could send him to purchase.'

Lobjang told everything in a single sentence as if, she will be unable to utter a single word as she stops.

'Yes…yes… why not? Mama, please give milk to Lobjangji. If anything else, please don't hesitate Lobjangji.'

Devyani asked out of courtesy.

'No Madaam, rest is there. Only one request more, if you can accommodate him to sleep in Deepesh's room, I shall be thankful. In my own room there is Pema's bed and other kitchen goods also. In the second room, we all use to sleep. My son-in-law may feel uneasy there. I know, it may be troublesome for you but a request…'

Lobjang was too polite.

'Well Lobjangji! No problem. Don't worry. There are two cots in Deepesh's room. Dhondhapji may sleep on one of them.'

Devyani solved her problem.

Lobjang went back, taking milk and then Deepesh burst out—

'What is this Didi? Why have you promised her to make him sleep in my room? These Tibetans don't take bath for months. There is bad smell from them all the time at distance also.'

'Keep quite! You talk without thought based on rumours. Who says that they don't take bath for months? In India, can anyone pass all seasons without taking a bath… is it possible? Is India Tibet, that everywhere ice is frozen and too much cold is here? There in Tibet also, except in a few areas, the seasons are almost like ours.'

Devyani gave short lecture to Deepesh.

'Well…well..don't advocate them. You are doing service there so everything of theirs appears flawless to you.'

Deepesh murmured in a low voice out of anger.

Devyani laughed at his innocence.

'This is not the reason Deepesh that I am observing their goodness because I do service in that institution rather I keep my eyes open to their short comings also, but it does not mean that we must stop eating, and have mutual friendship with them.'

'No. no, why will you stop your eating with them? Go and eat Momo[1] with them. Drink Chhang.[2]

Deepesh was murmuring like a small boy.

'Look Mama, what this Deepesh is saying. Cynical boy.'

Devyani laughed at Deepesh and moved ahead to arrange the bed of Tanchu Dhondhap.

'I will not sleep with him. Whosoever among you and Mama like to sleep with him, may sleep.'

Deepesh ultimately gave his decision to his mother.

'Try to understand someone's problem Deepesh. Poor Lobjang, how she has requested. This house is hers. We are tenants. If she did not give her house on rent, then?'

Mama tried to make him understand.

'Then, what she eats? It is not obligatory to each of us.'

'Sh….sh… keep quite! Perhaps he is coming. If he hears us, what he will think that we talk about guests like this?'

Mama tapped her forehead slowly. Deepesh threw himself on the bed out of anger.

'Oh, come….come Dhondhapji. Look, how we have taken shelter in your in-law's house.'

Devyani said politely when she saw Dhondhap coming with Lobjang.

Dhondhap also shown his gentleness and replied—

'No Didi! you people have given us shelter in your country. What we can give you in respect to that? Nothing.'

'Lo…you have turned the table.'

Laughingly she said. She enjoyed being addressed as Didi by Dhondhap. Although he was of the same age as she was, but this address had made him worthy of her affection as a younger one. Dragging the stool herself she sat on it. Dhondhap took his seat on the bed keeping his legs on the floor. Lobjang also sat on a chair.

---

1. Momo- A special dish made of meat of buffalo or cow.
2. Chhang- A kind of Tibetan wine made of barley.

'How should I welcome you Dhondhapji.' Devyani aksed affectionately. A smile was playing on her lips.

'Nothing Didi! Having my meal I moved from the guest house. Only one kindness I want from you.'

'What'?

'If I am telling you Didi then you also don't keep distance by calling me 'Aap' the elderly address.'

He did laugh with folded hands.

'O.K. Since now, only Dhondhap. Well?'

She was ashamed a little.

Mama also came from the next room and sat on the bed.

'Where is Deepesh mama?'

Devyani felt upset by Deepesh's behaviour. He had not come to his room yet.

'Perhaps he went to sleep.'

Mama was hesitant.

'Oh, Deepesh Bhaia[1]slept so soon? Does he not study at night?'

When Lobjang put her curiosity before, Devyani had to pretend—

'Actually, he felt a head-ache today.'

'We have made trouble for you Didi?'

Dhondhap said in formality.

'No, no, how trouble son? Don't think so. Take it easy. We are like one family here my son. You sleep without any worry.'

Mother abruptly said before Devyani.

'Where to sleep mama? I have to prepare an agenda of meeting tonight and so I have to be awake for a few hours.'

Dhondhap put his yellow coloured bag near the pillow on the bed and brought out his glasses from his pocket.

'Is your meeting there tomorrow too?'

Devyani was eager to know.

'Yes Didi! it will go-on for three days.'

'Where are the persons coming from?'

---

1. Bhaia- Brother in Hindi language.

'Where ever in the world, we are, ….some representatives from there and some local supporters.'

'Means?'

Devyani's curiosity increased.

'That is why I tell you that we owe a great debt of gratefulness to you. We have got the support of the local people of India also. In this supporting-Committee there are many local members who inspire our non-violent freedom-movement by their guidance and suggestions. Besides this, they give information about our mission to the Government of India as well as to the other countries of the world through their letters and articles, and thus create moral pressure on them.'

Dhondhap made his motto clear.

'Do you believe that this will make better effect?'

Devyani was taking interest in knowing their mission. We never break the loving silence of peace.

'Certainly it will influence. In the beginning we were alone but now, local people also are supporting as. It is for this reason also that our movement is completely non-violent. In our programmes, we never use even unparliamentary language for the Chinese rulers and others. Love and compassion for everybody is the basis of our mission.'

Dhondhap was explaining and Devyani was listening seriously. Lobjang and mama also were looking towards them with curiosity.

'You think yourself Didi, Lord Buddha had preached that hatred can't be removed by hatred but only through love is it possible, and usually what happens, there is lack of respect for non-violence itself in human beings. It is because of that the world's attention cannot be drawn towards non-violence easily. It is essential for this reason also that first we unite the persons having faith in non-violence on a world-level and then proceed forward with our mission.'

'But what do you think Dhondhap that only by the union of those persons, who have faith in non-violence, your mission will be successful? After observing the destructive result of the second world-war, to save the earth from a third world war, The United Nation was founded. No doubt, it was a ray of hope in deep darkness. But within half century of its establishment, the battles among different races and countries have denied its existence. There are wars and denial of human rights openly.'

Devyani threw a question.

'You are absolutely right Didi. It proves that the world is not suffering from lack of intellect, property or material things, but even then why the whole humanity is groaning with pain? What is it that the world lacks that makes a man violent? The answer is crystal clear— man will get peace when he progresses spiritually along with materialistic progress. There must be a balance between his spiritual and worldly progress for permanent peace. Actually man's real sorrow is a lack of spirituality for which he always wanders but due to ignorance he searches for it in worldly affairs.'

'Dhondhap, You are a philosopher also.'

Devyani was impressed by his thoughts.

'No Didi, I am only a simple and small worker. I believe in the theory that neutrality is always a helper of cruelty and it never helps the victimized person. Silence on exploitation always encourages injustice. It never encourages the victim of exploitation. On this very basis we have decided to awaken such type of neutral persons. We want to break their silence so that our exploitation may be stopped. The morale of the wrong party should fall down.'

Dhondhap explained his aim.

'Our best wishes are with you people and with your mission too. What is the main agenda of this meeting?'

Devyani asked.

'We are planning to send an appeal to the Chinese rulers and international organizations too with the collective signature of our local supporters who have joined this non-violent mission. There will be intellectuals, literary persons, artists etc in it so that a moral pressure can be made. This programme is taking shape in other countries also where Tibetan refugees are residing. We are taking the support of magazines and news papers so that information may spread on a large scale.'

'How is our…… means India's support?

Devyani wanted to know.

'Very positive Didi. We and our hundreds of coming generations too cannot pay off this debt.'

He became emotional.

'Do you ever think Dhondhap in this direction too that you must go to Tibet and fight there for your rights? As you can see, happened with the Indian freedom movement?'

'It was experimented once Devyani Madam. At that time I was in Dharmshala. A group of Tibetan fighters was ready to go to their country but the Indian Army had stopped them on its border itself.'

This time Lobjang replied to Devyani.

'Why? Why they were stopped?'

This was a new fact for Devyani.

'Because China came to know about the plan. As you know that Chinese spies are everywhere. Our small activities are also reaching them. That is why they pressurized the Government of India by saying that it is not proper and in favour of India that Tibetan refugees should conduct their movement of separation from there. It must be stopped. So, the Indian Army did not allow them to go to Tibet.'

'It means if these Tibetan refugees want to go back now to their country, they can't do so?'

Deepesh also came and sat among them a few moments before. He spoke out suddenly.

'No, why not they will go? They often go but as single or two three persons at a time. But the administration in Tibet watches those persons who have arrived from a foreign country. That person's activities and conduct both are being observed, whether he is provoking or engaged in any anti-administrative activities or not? If everything is found normal, that person can live easily in Tibet.'

Dhondhap replied.

'Then why is there an objection to these Tibetans living there in Tibet? If they let them live peacefully?'

This question of Deepesh was somehow bitter-tasted.

'It is not so brother. They behave in other ways with the ladies, children and Lamas.'

Dhondhap was in a dejected mood. His voice was full of sorrow.

'Our girls are forcibly being married with them so that our race itself may be finished. If a baby is born somewhere, the girl-child is being killed and if it is a male-baby, he is snatched and after sometimes he is recruited in the Chinese Force. You think, if we are Tibetans, we would want to marry Tibetans or with them?'

The answer made Deepesh silent this time.

'You are absolutely right Lobjang ji. Now we must stop this discussion here because it is late at night.'

Devyani wanted to stop the discussion because of Deepesh's behaviour.

'You will sleep here Deepesh, isn't it?'

Dhondhap asked formally.

'No, you have yet to write and I feel a head-ache today. So, we all shall sleep in the next room.'

Saying it Deepesh turned towards the next room.

'You take it easy Dhondhap. We shall sleep together there. Goodnight.'

Devyani had filled the gap of Deepesh' roughness with her affection.

'O.K. Didi. Sorry for the trouble.'

He smiled.

'Oh, don't be so formal Dhondhap. Goodnight.'

She also went to the next room.

Deepesh was arranging a bed for himself on the floor. He was murmuring slowly while spreading the bed sheet on the mattress.

'Why they will go now? Very often they organize their meetings and show that they are fighting for freedom. Actually, they have become habitual of getting so many facilities here in India so why will they want to go back to Tibet? Will they like to move in hilly Tibet riding on mules or by foot itself? Here they are taking the privilege of A.C. rooms and enjoying beautiful cars.'

'Only a few Tibetans might be getting the pleasure of A.C. rooms here but there, in Tibet, the complete atmosphere of nature is better than air conditioning. This is the reason that most of them expire, leaving Tibet.'

Sitting on her cot Devyani said. She was wrapping her long hair in the shape of a bun.

'Didi, you ask your Geshe Jampaji some day that whether he too is making up his mind to go to Tibet?'

Deepesh laid down on his bed.

'May God provide them that day of freedom, of course he would love to go.'

The serious and sober face of Geshe Jampa flashed before Devyani's eyes.

'Then, what you will do Didi?'

Deepesh did laugh loudly.

'What do you mean?'

Devyanin took another meaning of his words.

'I mean, to whom will you teach then? Free from your service…?'

'Dam it…. I thought….'

She became puzzled and could not think what she should say.

'Do one thing Didi!'

Deepesh whispered in joking mood. Devyani was listening to him with a smile.

'You capture that monastery by converting yourself into a lady monk in the same way. Only you would have to cut these beautiful hair.'

Deepesh was still joking.

'Mama, look at this silly boy. He never understands that what should be said and what not? Just before sometime, how he was talking with Dhondhap? It seemed that all the Tibetan refugees are sitting on his head. He has a big responsibility for those people.'

Laying on her bed Devyani was saying with a smile and satire too. She remembered hair-less lady monk Dolma. When she was reminded, Geshe Jampa's glimpse was also along with her.

'See Didi, the time will come. China has captured Tibet and these people will make their colony in India in the future. They can't be removed from here. If the Indian Government will not be alert, they will demand a piece of land for themselves in India in the name of human rights. The relation with China is also getting bitter day by day, and this is another issue.'

Deepesh was grumbling still.

'Oh, please keep quite my foreign minister! Only you know all the policies and future of India? Kindly go to sleep. The walls also have ears.'

Using a sweet scolding she changes her side on the bed.

'There are ears in the walls also for them but we people have walls standing in front of our eyes. The population of our country is increasing so speedily on the one hand and above it these refugees also….. and there…… those Chakma[1]- Chakmi …. Another big problem. What have been to us? Always we sleep and sleep and then try to awake when things have gone wrong.'

Deepesh again whispered towards Devyani's ears and she did laugh.

'Hey….' Bharat Bhagy Vidhata,[2] please take sleep so that you can awake at the right time.'

Devyani told him by turning her face towards Deepesh.

'What can I do by awaking also when you older people are filled with Tibetan love and overflowing it.'

---

1. Chakma- Refugees from Bangladesh taking shelter in India.
2. Line of Indian national anthem.

Deepesh too laughingly said and pretended to sleep.

A sweet smile danced on the lips of Devyani. She was reminded of that incident—

'Language is an essential attribute for love. Love cannot bud in one's heart for other language-speaking person so soon as it buds for own language-speaking person.'

There was a discussion on true love going on in the teachers room. In this reference Devyani was keeping her view seriously.

'There are many faces of love, aren't there? First of all we should explain its traits and forms.'

When Naveen Sharma had put this idea, everybody laughed loudly.

'You are doing cuts and pieces of love just like the practical examination of science of Intermediate class, my dear friend Naveen.'

Balendu told laughingly.

'It is very necessary sir. Normally the frog of love crooks itself but after your cutting and shutting also if it can crook again in the same manner, then you think yourself successful in love.'

'Oh, now Naveen's thought is turning towards ugliness. I am going to take class.'

Devyani stood up suddenly.'

Geshe Jampa was seen coming from that side as she came out from the teachers' room. His serious and sober gait and thinking eyes as if always lost in some serious thought could attract anybody.

Will there have been love too budding into his innerself for someone? If Natural human weaknesses would have peeped into his heart then how could he get rid of it? Very difficult like his Mukti-Sadhna.[1] Thinking it Devyani had reached close to Geshe Jampa and looking at him she even forgot to wish him.

'What is the matter Devyani? Any problem…..?'

He stayed for a moment and asked.

---

1. Mukti-Sadhna- Freedom movement of Tibetans.

Devyani was astonished suddenly as if she had been caught red-handed.

'Tashi Delek, Gela.'

She folded her hands to wish him.

'What are you contemplating Devyani?'

Geshe Jampa again repeated his question.

'No, nothing Gela.'

She wiped her face with the edge of her Saree and replied.

'There is no need of any language for expression of love, hatred and confusion. The face itself reveals it.'

Saying it, Geshe Jampa took a deep look at her.

She found herself unable to look towards him straight forward. Looking towards the flower-pot placed in the verandah she replied—

'Yes sir, just I was thinking about…. there was a discussion going on and I was thinking over it.'

Her sentence was broken.

'Any harsh topic….?' Geshe Jampa was in a mood to talk to her.

'No sir, nothing like that.'

'If anytime it is, don't hesitate to inform me.'

'Yes sir.' She bent her head out of respect.

'Do you have a class?'

'Yes sir.'

'O.K.'

He moved ahead. Belendu and Naveen also came out from the teacher's room. They were unaware of Geshe Jampa's presence in the verandah. She also started to move hearing their foot-steps.

'Platonic theory of love.'

They were discussing yet. The words buzzed into the ears of Devyani and Geshe Jampa together and they tried to see Balendu and Naveen at the same time turning their heads. In this process the eyes of Devyani and Geshe Jampa were brought together once again and unknowingly a sweet smile floated on the lips of both of them.

Thinking about that sweet incident, sleep had captured her eyes softly. So many rainbows started dancing in the silence of night.

7

'Maai, may I come in?' Removing the silken yellow curtain on one side of Dolma's room Devyani asked.

'Yes, Devyani please come.'

Dolma's weak voice came out from inside the room and Devyani was astonished.

'What happened Maai? Are you well? Why have you called me?'

Devyani's several questions resounded together in the room. She went near Dolma's bed and sat on a stool. There were a few medicines the other stool beside the bed.

'Maai Lama Migmar had gone to call me. Is your problem becoming more serious?'

'No, it is better but too much weakness is the main problem. If I move even four or five steps, my breathing problem increases.'

Dolma was breathing heavily.

'What to do, give me a task Maai.'

'Nothing to do my daughter! Only you have to go with these children to the Tibetan Research Centre. Losar[1] is being celebrated there. I used to go there every year with them.'

'But Maai, it will continue till late at night?'

'That is why I am of the opinion that some responsible person must be with them. They are kids. If it was during the day time, I could send them with Migmar.'

'Will Geshe Jampa sir not go there?'

All of sudden Devyani asked. She herself was unable to understand, why she asked so.

---

1.   Losar- Tibetan New Year

Dolma was telling her without grasping the deep meaning of her sentence—

'Actually he is head. He does not participate in such types of festivals.'

'Why? Is there any such custom in your society?'

'No, Devyani, no custom is like this. Only for this reason that first, we should always remember our dependence that we are refugees in this country and secondly if senior officers will participate in the festivals, the youth and children can't enjoy freely. They will feel some restriction. So, every year on this special occasion Geshe Jampa used to go out somewhere else or live in the city so that one cannot feel any restriction.'

'Oh, this is also a kind of penance.'

A sentence with a deep sigh came out from Devyani's mouth.

'What can we do my dear, if we are born in such a crucial time, we have to face all these agonies. We must sacrifice our amusement too.'

Dolma was looking towards the roof.

'Is there any destitute?'

'You are right my daughter! That, there is no destitute but it is in the same way as if there is a worthy son, then, to think about family becomes his moral duty but if he is unworthy, he is not responsible for anyone and all the happiness of the world is for him. No feeling of responsibility. You can understand this example.'

Dolma was looking at Devyani's face.

'But Maai, you do go in Losar. You are older than him and overburdened with responsibilities too.'

Devyani tried to make the atmosphere light. Her eyes were laughing and lips were slightly curved with a smile.

'I am Maai of all children, means their mother. A woman who is everything for children but nothing in herself. Her existence is just like water. It takes several shapes time to time but Geshe Jampa is holding an important post. One cannot give shape to his existence according to one's will. It is neither proper, nor can be done. The great responsibility that has been taken by him, cannot be thrown out. It can be the main cause of disrepute. There is a fear to fall down in society's eyes as well as in his own also.'

'This time, has he gone somewhere else or is in this very city?'

Devyani's question was neat and clean.

'Only you are being told that he is very much here, otherwise everyone knows that he has gone to Rajghat.'

Dolma whispered into Devyani's ear.

'Can I meet him?'

'Perhaps, he will not meet.'

'Why? I'll keep it a secret.'

She also whispered.

' The guard will not allow you.' Dolma made it clear.

'The guard might be knowing that you are well aware of Gela?'

Maai Dolma said again.

'Yes, he knows. Then, you instruct the guard that he should let me meet Gela.'

'But, why do you want so?'

'Only I want to wish him Tibetan new year. Perhaps he might be hiding himself from the sight of Tibetan students and people on this very occasion but I don't think that the same will be with me also. I can give him good wishes at least for this.'

'I suspect, whether he may not be unhappy.'

There was a confusion in Dolma's voice.

'I am also his subordinate. If I will see he is upset, I shall beg his pardon. I'll make it clear also that I came on my insistence.'

'Look, try once. If the guard allows you to meet, you can do.'

Dolma permitted her.

'Which Tibetan year is this Maai?'

'Tello[1].

'O.K. Maai! I'll come tomorrow evening to take the children there. Today I am going to wish Gela.'

---

1. Tello-Tibetan name.

She stood up. The lady monk was watching Devyani very carefully. She was unable to understand that why someone else had not wished Geshe Jampa in this way like Devyani?'

'May I go Maai?'

Devyani was seeking permission.

'Are you in hurry Devyani?'

Dolma threw a question in reply to her question.

'No, no Maai, there is no hurry.'

Devyani sat again with shyness. She became conscious as if Maai would have co-related it with Geshe Jampa.

'Sit for a while more. My sickness has been lessened as I feel, talking with you.'

A little smile danced there on the weak face of Dolma.

'Madam, may I go?'

Peeping through door, Lama Migmar was asking. He was still standing outside the room.

'Oh yes, yes…. You may go Lama. I forgot that you are standing outside.

Devyani replied—

'If you want to sit here, you can sit Migmar.'

Dolma indicated towards the chair.

'No Maai, I want to go. Some urgent work is there.'

'Well.'

Seeking Dolma's permission, Migmar went.

'My heart feels distressed seeing them in monk-dresses at such an early age Maai.'

'Why, It is the subject of sacrifice and austerity.'

Dolma made it clear.

'Yet, to detach from the worldly affairs at such a tender age is quite troublesome Maai, as I think.'

'It is prestigious in our society. There, at least one child of the family becomes a monk by necessity.'

Dolma told with pride.

'But Maai, excuse me, one thing I want to ask— do the human weaknesses disappear from the mind of each and every monk?'

A very complicated question was thrown before Dolma to be answered.

Dolma was silent for few moments and then replied slowly—

'If one is a human being, then its weaknesses also will be there but to conquer these weaknesses through austerity and self control is the main goal of this path. If someone is defeated to overcome it, then another path is also open to him. He or she can adopt it. There is no unbreakable wall that can't be crossed from this side to that.'

'In our country Grihasth Ashram[1] is placed higher and it has been told that this life is also a true austerity. To lead the life of four Ashramas[2] are compulsory in one's life. These four Ashramas are the different stages of life and to lead the life according to these stages is essential for human conduct. I think, nowhere in the world, there is such a scientific division of human life. Far from all extremes.'

'Devyani, I think, religion is always influenced by time, space and circumstances. These very doctrines of the Tathagat spread out in some other way in Tibet and it had changed its nature more or less in other countries too. When I came to India, I developed a new thought. I recognized religion in its true sense. Far away from every Tantra and Mantra.'

There was a feeling of peace in Dolma's eyes.

'Maai, one thing I ask, if you don't mind.'

There was a glimpse of a smile too along with begging excused on the face of Devyani. Both her hands were folded.

'Yes ask Devyani, don't hesitate.'

Dolma caught her hands in her both hands and assured with affection.

---

1. Grihasth Ashram- Family life in Hindu religion.
2. Ashrama-There are four stages in life that is called 'Ashram' in Hindu religion- (i) Brahmcharya, (ii) Grihasth, (iii) Vaanprasth (iv) Samnyas.

'I feel respect along with curiosity also to peep in your life Maai.'

Devyani was preparing herself to ask something.

Dolma was smiling to see her.

'When did you become a monk?'

She questioned.

'I was of your age that is at present.'

Dolma's voice was calm and quite.

'Why? Was the attachment with life finished all of sudden?'

'It is a complicated question my daughter! I'll give you the answer some day later. Not today.'

Dolma put her hands lifelessly in the lap of Devyani, in which there was affection and helplessness both.

'Well Maai, I'll ask later when your health will be O.K. Today, tell me only one thing, whether you became a monk after coming to India or before it…?'

Devyani was anxious to know.

'I came here after deciding it.'

A short answer of Dolma raised many questions in Devyani's mind, but it was not the proper time to ask.

'Oh!'

Only one word came out from Devyani's throat and there spread a silence in the room for some time. Devyani began to tickle gently the hands of Dolma laying in her lap.

'Should I move Maai now? Again I'll sit with you some day and turn over the pages of your past life.'

Devyani smiled.

'Why do you want to turn over the pages? Any special aim?'

Dolma's creeping smile was weak.

'Nothing very special. Only I am curious to know about you, about Gela, rather to say, about all Tibetans because there is a different story written in everyone's past life. I want to read those very stories.'

Dolma laughed as Devyani explained it with innocence.

'I to have pasted many pages of my life with each other so that they cannot be opened fluttering with the wind. Now, how can you read my complete story?'

'I shall guess the middle part of the story by hearing its opening and closing.'

'Yet, the story will not be completed.'

There was a child like laughter on Dolma's lips.

'I'll try my best that I can read the whole story by separating the pages with softness.'

Devyani also became agile.

'You are a naughty girl.'

Dolma rebuked her with affection.

'O.K. Maai, I move from here. See, if I can meet Gela.'

Laughingly she stood up and folded her hands to wish Maai Dolma.

8

The room of Dolma become quiet as Devyani went from there. Dolma closed her eyes and her expanded past gathered together and shrank into two aquatic-shells.

'Loye, O Loye!'

Her best friend Pasang had come hastily to her. Her scarf was trembling yet hanging behind. The long necklace of pearl was crooked in it.

'What is the matter, Pasang! Why are you gasping? Have you seen ghost or devil?'

Loye asked sitting on the mound of small rocks and sands on the bank of Kyuchhu river.

The yaks were grazing in the green field. The frontal hill was covered with wild roses and gooseberry. Beside that hill, a huge building was under construction. Tibetan labourers of Loye's village named Fun-Do had told others were working there along with the Chinese officers.

Shyu-Shing-Hu had told Loye one day—

'We are establishing here a big plant. Many scientists will come here to work.'

'Will our people also?'

Loye asked with suspicion.

'Yes, yes, why not? Whosoever is qualified, he will be kept accordingly here in service. Our Government is of this very opinion that Tibetans must leave their torpor and join the progressive outlook. They can move with the world step by step.'

Shyu-Shing-Hu looked at Loye with love and explained the planning of the Chinese Government.

'Then why are you people being opposed? Tibetan people are of the opinion that your intention is not right.'

'Do you also think that my intention is not good?'

He asked with affection.

'No…. I don't know….. what can I know?'

She was entangled in her own answer. Shyu-Shing-Hu laughed on her innocence.

Very often Loye used to come with her yaks to graze on this bank of Kyuchhu river. The yaks used to graze in the sloping field of hill and she used to look at the frontal greenery and listen to the rippling sound of the flowing river with enchantment. Sometimes a group of butter-vendors used to pass on from that side with their yaks in the valley, then, she used to be more enchanted. It seemed as if in a painting of nature life is also roaming.

On that day her heart beating increased out of fear when Shyu-Shing-Hu came and stood in front of her for the first time.

'Yes,….' She suddenly stood up at her own place. Her voice was trembling.

'Don't be afraid. I am not a robber. My name is Shyu-Shing-Hu. There is my camp in front of this place. Is there any shop where eatable things may be available? I want to purchase.'

When he explained his motto, she was assured.

'What do you want?'

She asked, looking him seriously.

'Everything, means tea, butter, jyupa, meat, Chhang etc….'

He reckoned. She saw him with surprise.

'Do you have nothing?'

Shyu-Shing-Hu did laugh at her question. Laughingly he said—

'No, I have a little but if we have to stay here for a long time, the place must be known. It will be purchased when finished.'

'It is beside my house at Fun-Do. They bring all the goods from Lhasa. The people of my village Fun-Do use to buy from there.'

She explained him.

'Will you show me the way to that shop?'

She was hesitant of his proposal. What will the people of her village think? God knows how they will react to see her with a unknown person who belongs to her enemy's-community too?

'What have you started to think?'

'Oh, nothing, you can go along the shore on that side and then turn right. There, you can see that stream bend,…. is bigger than it, there is a hill covered with bushes… in the valley of that hill, there are fields… mustard-flowers in it… yellow, yellow…. at present… the path goes through these fields. You can reach easily. You can find the foot-prints of yaks also on the way. After some distance there you will find two buildings almost like ruins. Nobody lives in them. The walls are made of rocks. As soon as you will see those buildings, just think that you are about to reach. You will understand that shop is very near.'

She was demonstrating the way to Shyu-Shing-Hu by raising her hand to the wind and there was a soft smile on the lips of Shyu-Shing-Hu.

'Oh, are you telling me the shop of butter or sending me to Mongolia?'

He laughed loudly.

She giggled. To avoid her shyness, she pretended—

'Actually I can't go with you just now. My yaks have not filled their stomach with grass. I'll have to go home after they have grazed.'

'Do you come here daily with these yaks?'

'Yes, but why?'

'Then, I shall go with you some other day to know the way. I can't reach alone thus.'

A sweet mischief was on his lips.

'O Loye! What you are thinking? You are looking towards me and your mind is somewhere else.'

Pasang shuddered Loye. Loye startled and came into her present. Shyu-Shing-Hu disappeared from her mind. Hiding her feeling, she told Pasang-

'I was thinking that if your would be bridegroom may come at present and only one...'

'O.K., o.k., leave me, think about yourself. Bar-mi[1] has come for you from the village Sakya. Long-Chang[2] also came before your family. Now you go to Dong-Mo-la of village Sakya and there you graze yaks.'

Pasang laughed loudly. She sat very near to Loye.

"Truely?"

Loye was asking.

'Then, do you think false? The uncle of the bridegroom is sitting yet in your house. He is Bar-mi. Should I call him here?'

Pasang said in a mischievous voice playing with the edge of her scarf.

'No, no. I did not mean that....'

'Yes, you use to graze the yaks in this valley and there everything will be done. It may be also that you will be sent to village Sakya, your in-law's house, from here itself carried on a mule. What is the matter to worry dear friend?'

Pasang was joking.

And really her marriage was arranged instantaneously. Her horoscope matched with Jigme. All the relatives were gathered together one night before the marriage at her house. Some persons came from the bridegroom's side also. After dancing and musical programme and dinner, early in the morning, they moved for Jigme's village Sakya along with Loye. She was told that Jigme had three brothers. By being eldest among them, Loye had to look after the whole family. The luggage of Loye was loaded in a Kwa[3] at the bank of Kyuchhu river. They crossed the river one after another. The animals with them crossed the river by swimming in it. The sky was covered with clouds. Crossing the frontal stream trend they climbed from right side. The hill was covered with bushes

---

1. Bar-mi-The mediator in Tibetan marriage.
2. Long-Chang- Wine given for the proposal of marriage in Tibetan custom.
3. Kwa- A boat made of leather.

and wild grass. The smoke was raising higher coming out from the camps of Dokpa people on the other side of the river. Some children were running behind their yaks.

Loye looked everywhere with deep frustration. She found a few fields of barley there also. The old narrow pathway between the fields indicated that there were plenty of fields long back. The trees of cedar seemed to stand in ceremonious welcome to her. Here must be the camp of Shyu-Shing-Hu somewhere, that she used to see from that side of the river, Loye thought. Her heart craved for him. The frustrated eyes of Shyu-Shing-Hu seemed to question her—

'You have not awaited me?'

Tears fell down from Loye's eyes.

'Don't weep daughter. Your in-law's house is very near to your own house.Whenever you will wish to go, Jigme will help you to reach there. He is a very gentle boy. They are three brothers. All of them are engaged in the butter business. There is want of nothing.'

Moving side by side to her, Barmi uncle began to console, watching her tears. He thought that Loye was afraid of the new and unknown in-law's family.

Loye rubbed her eyes with the golden scarf hanging from her head. The marriage party stayed for sometime in that valley to take rest. Each one came down from his mule when white-dressed rider holding Sipaho[1] in his hands came down from his white mare. Loye also bent-headed sat on a mat spread-out behind a rock.

Mother and father had come to give their farewel to them upto the bank of Kyuchhu river. After that they went back. Younger brother Sonam was with her. Mother embraced Loye and told in choked voice—

'Go Loye, be happy there. Don't worry about here. Keep your husband and his family with affection. Don't think about any other problem. Everything will be O.K.'

---

1. Sipaho-A symbol to avoid the evil spirits.

Loye could understand the worries of her mother. Clinging with her mother her sorrows broke the limits and sobbings turned into an ocean of tears.

'Mama, if Shyu comes, please don't let anyone misbehave with him. You make him to understand everything in private.'

She was requesting her mother in between the sobbings.

'Don't bother about it my daughter. I'll manage everything. He is wise enough and will understand everything— our circumstances and your helplessness.'

Mother whispered with grief.

'Mama, he is very emotional. May not take any wrong-step. My heart is troubled to think about it.'

She said slowly and wept bitterly.

'No daughter, I myself will make him understand. He will not take any wrong decision. I promise you. Only, you be conscious about it and don't give any clue to your in-laws, otherwise your life will be turned into hell.'

Mother assured her and made her ride on the mare.

Butter-mixed tea was served before everybody. Taking first sip of it, Shyu-Shing-Hu again was reminded of her. Pretending to see the shop of butter, he came to her house for the first time.

'Mama, this is Shyu-Shing-Hu. He is supervisor in that plant that is going to be established across the river.'

Loye introduced him to her mother. Mother threw a suspicious look on him. Loye understood. The guest must not be insulted, so she suddenly did said—

'He did not know the way to the shop nearby our house, so I accompanied him.'

'O.K., please sit my son.'

Mother's voice was very formal. Loye felt uneasy.

'Would you like to take tea?'

She became reckless. She presumed that this proposal must come from mother's side but contrary to it, mother's enquiry and investigating eyes with formal behaviour made Loye humiliated. She felt as if she insulted Shyu-Shing-Huby bringing him here.

'Yes, yes, why not? If you also will take.'

Shyu handled the situation with softness.

'I just bring.'

Loye turned towards kitchen. Shyu sat on the wooden cot till then. Mother also went to the kitchen behind Loye.

'How are you acquainted with this fellow? He is not Tibetan?'

Mother starred with angry eyes.

'Mama, this poor chap.... he was wandering, only I brought him to show the path. Nothing else.'

'But a Chinese.... Do you not know how it will he be taken in our society? Do you want to crush our prestige to dust?'

Mother became aggressive.

'Are all the Chinese bad and all the Tibetans good mama!'

Her protesting voice was resonant.

'Keep silence, it is in your favour that your father is not in the house otherwise you can imagine his anger. Give him tea and make him depart from here as soon as possible.'

Mother was controlling her anger anyhow.

'Then, what do you think that have I brought him here by invitation to stay two three months?'

She laughed loudly. Mother also could not control her laughter. Hiding it she went to the next room and sat on a stool beside Shyu-Shing-Hu.

Loye also went to that room taking Masung[1] and butter mixed tea in an engraved cup. There was an easy dialogue going on between her mother and Shyu. Mama's displeasure had disappeared. In between she used to look outside the door, perhaps to know about father's arrival. This time she also wanted that father would not come. She was influenced by the cognate behaviour of Shyu and did not want that this gentle boy feel any kind of humiliation from her husband.

---

1. Masung-An eatable thing like cake.

If father would have come, his questions may hurt Shyu and he could not forget that insult.

'Please, have your tea son.'

Mother gave a cup of tea to him. Loye was standing there taking support of the door. She held her cup in her hand and was listening to Shyu very carefully.

'Mama, some time you please come to my camp also. I am far away from my own mother and that lack seems to have been filled as I met you.'

Shyu had taken a sip of tea. Mother smiled. Loye had seen the smile as soft as butter on mother's face. There looked as if a thin stream of affection for Shyu was in mother's eyes.

'Yes, I'll come someday my son. Actually, it is very rare that I go out of the house.'

She was telling him.

'Why, you give time to Loye daily to go outside and have no time for yourself? One day you make her to stay in the house.'

Loye tapped her forehead slowly out of perplexity. She was ashamed and astonished as Shyu had disclosed innocently the secrets of her meeting daily with him. Mother's back was towards her. Shyu saw her reaction but could not realize his fault. He was of the impression that Loye might have told everything to her family-members about him.

But when he saw Loye beating slowly her forehead on his foolishness, he got the point. Changing the topic he said—

'Mama, I myself shall come someday to bring you with me. Now, I have to come very often for purchasing from the shop nearby.'

He took a long sip so that tea may be finished in one go and in this process a sound came out from his lips. Loye did laugh.

'You people take a sip with the loud sound like this?' She said with laughter.

'Keep quite. All the time your buffoonery goes on.'

Mother rebuked her.

'Really mama, you are right. To move with unknown persons in this way, to make fun of them, it does not suit a Tibetan girl. Is that not so mama?'

A naughty smile was playing on the Shyu's lips also.

'What have you told? I brought you with me to show the path and contrary to it you started preaching to me? Oh world! it is not for gentle people.'

Loye had shown her artificial anger with sweet surprise. She was a bit confused by such dialogues of Shyu.

'A person is deceived in doing goodness itself sometimes. Isn't it mama? Suppose, anyone mislead her?'

He said.

'You are right son! She is unaware of worldly affairs till now.

Mother joined his voice.

'Well, someone would mislead me and I would start to go with him holding his finger like a child? Am I foolish that I'll go with anyone?'

Loye reacted.

'Then, am I foolish that I came here with you'

He was laughing.

'No, it was your need so I accompanied you to show the way up to here.'

'If I did accompany you like this to show the way to my house, then?'

'What did I mean with your house? I would never go?' A sweet quarrel was going on between them.

Although, mother was not displeased by the sarcasm of both but a mark of worry could be seen on her forehead.

Loye was remembering Shyu.

After a short rest, the marriage party again moved towards Sakya. Loye also rode on her decorated mare after searching the presence of Shyu-Shing-Hu with her desolated eyes. Her mind was full of agony. She remembered Shyu too much. Perhaps he might not be knowing that all this will happen within one month.

His innocence and simplicity was crushed under his cast. How confidently he spoke that day, when, returning from her house, Loye asked him with anger—

'Why have you disclosed to mama that I used to meet you earlier too?'

'To hide anything means there is improbity in the corner of one's heart. I cannot burden my soul. The pleasure that one can feel in being transparent, can't found in hiding. I don't want to hide my relation with you.'

Shyu had said sitting beside her on the bank of Kyucchu.

'I did not mean that it should be hidden, but only wanted to let the proper time come.

'No time is improper. Only the intention or deed of a person may be improper. I love you with my pure heart and want to accept you in my life forever. For this, I don't have to wait for another time, nor any kind of abstinence from the present time. I am coming tomorrow to talk to your father in this regard.'

She was frightened watching Shyu's firmness.

'You don't know my father. He is very rigid. He will like to kill me but will not give my hand to a Chinese…..'

Her voice was trembling.

'Neither to be a Chinese is my fault, nor to love you either. Why should we crush our emotions due to the political scenario of the country? Why should we lead a life of suffocation?'

'But who will understand our emotions Shyu?'

Loye beseeched in an humble manner before him.

'Your father and my mama….'

And exactly on the next day Shyu reached her house in the morning. Mother was stunned when Shyu had put his proposal directly before father—

'Father, I want to make Loye my life-partner. I hope, you will not refuse.'

Father was shocked for a while. He did not expect for such a proposal from an unknown person.

It was a few minutes ago that mother had given the introduction of Shyu—

'This is Shyu. He is supervisor. In that plant….. which is being constructed across the river.'

'Well, O.K., how did you come here?'

Father was gazing at him with angry eyes and without care Shyu put his proposal before him.

Loye's heart-beating increased as she had hid herself behind the door. Holding her breath she was trying to listen to the answer of her father.

He was replying as chewing his each word—

'Till now, you people were forcibly finishing us and now you bring the proposals also by entering our houses?'

'Please father, don't weigh our emotions with your political eyes. I put this proposal with the complete purity of my heart.'

Shyu-Shing-Hu also seemed firm in his dialogue.

'This is the part of your policy Mr. that anyhow the whole race of Tibetans must be removed so that the path may be clear forever.'

There was a disgust in the voice of father.

'You are taking me wrong father! I want Loye….'

'Stop, don't pronounce my daughter's name again. I'll think it better to cut Loye into pieces and throw them in the water of Kyuchhu. We can face any misery but will not let your intention be fulfilled. Now you may go and never come this side again.'

Father stood-up out of anger. The wrinkles of his forehead darkened more. Mother was silent. To say anything means invitation to a battle in the house.

Loye closed her eyes. Her mind seemed to be empty. The heart-beatings were out of control. She wanted to run and stand before Shyu-Shing-Hu, who was going back with deep sorrow. She wanted to trap him in her eyes. Who knows whether she can meet him again or not but the rigid face of her father stopped her steps. Her legs seemed frozen, where she was.

Next day she went hastily on the bank of Kyuchhu river when her father had gone outside for some time. She was hopeful that, may be, Shyu would come there to meet her. Her heart was beating out of fear. What will happen, if someone sees her there? It was morning time and people used to come that side very often.

Emotions had crossed the distance between hearts. Really Shyu was roaming on the bank of Kyuchhu in restlessness. A sweet wave of happiness floated on his face to see her there.

'I did not know 'why', but was assured that you will certainly come today at this time Loye! I reached here just a few minutes ago.'

Shyu-Shing-Hu came near to her.

'I was also helpless to stop myself. Perhaps hearts know the message of each other. I have to go at once. It will create problem if someone sees me here. I have come here to beg pardon for the misbehaviour of my father.'

She told with folded hands and her eyes were filled with tears.

'Why, again I became alien to you? Your father has become yours? Sirrah! Whatever the circumstances are existing in this country, any guardian can think so. Here, your father is not the defaulter.'

'How innocent and liberal you are! You accept your insult also so simply. This very simplicity of yours aggrieves me much more. I feel helpless Shyu! What should be done, I am unable to decide.'

Loye wept bitterly.

'No, you'll not weep Loye. I am going to my city Shinhava today itself. I promise you to come back soon. Don't be impatient. My mama will be with me. I am sure that she will be able to convince your father certainly. Only you wait for me, on this very bank of Kyuchhu. Did I know, that coming here for service I will be entangled in your love.'

Shyu tapped her cheeks with softness and affection.

Being astonished she moved one step back.

'No, please don't touch me Shyu. If someone will see, it can invite misfortune.'

She did whisper. Her doe-like eyes ran everywhere with fear. She became assured that no one had seen them.

'Now, you must go, I also proceed from here. I shall come to your house as soon as I come with my mother. In between, you remember me sometimes sitting on this bank of Kyuchhu. O.K.?'

He was saddened but tried to laugh.

'Yes.'

Her voice was choked. She could not speak anything further. Only she looked at Shyu for a few moments with tears and suddenly turned back sobbing. She could feel the soft touch of his affectionate eyes on her back for a long time.

But she was tied up with Jigme before Shyu come. Mother had requested her not to destroy their prestige in the society and on the other hand, father begged from her a small sacrifice for saving their culture and country. Helplessly she surrendered. She could tolerate everything but not to decorate her forehead with the mark of treason.

Crossing the miles of fields, they reached to Sakya village. There was a Jong[1] on the left peak of the hill. It seemed very beautiful. In the valley to the right side, the village was situated. Destroyed towers and ruins were indicating an inhabited place and population of the past but now a desert. Loye raised her eyes to survey the village properly. The ladies and gents were singing while harvesting the crop here and there. The valley was filled with the echoing of their songs. After going ahead on a slope they turned right on the way made of small rocks and stones. The village was very near but no mirth was there. Loye was not surprised. It was the normal nature of almost every village in Tibet. Even if a few people went out from one village to participate in any occasion, the whole village seemed like a desert.

Loye remembered Shyu's joke.

'Your customs and religion are responsible for making so many villages a desert.'

---

1. Jong-Fort.

'How?' Loye had asked.

'The custom of a single wife for a whole family. How do you feel Loye thinking about it? If you have to love too many persons at a time and together, then, how will you do justice with each?'

He laughed loudly. She became serious at his question.

'I fill with hatred to think it. I can't marry in a such family even if it is too influential.'

Loye peeped into his eyes with firmness.

'Oh, it means your intension about me is doubtful till now.'

'No, absolutely not so.'

She gave a vague answer to him and laughed loudly.

'If I'll allow you to fluctuate then…..'

Shyu also laughed leaving his sentence incomplete.

The marriage party reached at the door of Jigme now and still she was plunged in her past. Every ritual of outside the door was finished. Entering the house, a bulky lady garlanded her with a traditional necklace in which five coloured small flags were tied in the form of an arrow. She was brought to a decorated canopy and made to sit beside Jigme. This bulky lady was her mother-in-law. The custom of Chema-eating had been completed. Between the merriment of marriage her mother-in-law completed the last ritual of placing the scarf on the neck of Jigme and Loye. Loye's eyes were filled with tears repeatedly, while Jigme's eyes were lusty-red.

The same red glimpse was seen in his eyes at that day also when he came in the room intoxicated with Chhang and completely out of self. Laying down on the bed, he spoke—

'See, I have brought you by marrying so that you live with my three brothers together and properly. We shall not let you feel a lack of anything. But if you will try to deceive us, I'll send you to Fun-do after cutting off your nose. Understood?'

'Can there not be separate wife for each of your brothers?'

She was asking with fear.

There was a quarrel going on regarding this very issue between Jigme and her from last fifteen days. She was not ready to have the relation of wife with all of three brothers, while Jigme was rigid to this proposal from first night.

'Why this useless talk? Do you think that my property must be divided into pieces and it should be thrown before crows and vultures?'

He burst out in anger. Along with his eyes, his face also became red. For the first time Loye had seen Jigme's formidable face.

'But we have passed only few days of our married life. At least let one year be passed then…'

He interrupted—

'I don't believe in all these things. Neema is my twin-brother. How I can say to him that you wait for one year? Then I must say to my youngest brother that he would wait for more than two years?'

Jigme put his logic before Loye.

'Then, is there no meaning of my will or unwillingness in your eyes?'

A protest was floating in Loye's eyes too.

'Should I make you to understand our traditions in a new style? Had you not been told all this before marriage?'

Jigme's behaviour was arrogant.

'No, none had told me about this condition otherwise I would had rejected this marriage itself.'

Enraged she stood up on her place.

'Might you have gone then with that culprit Shyu-Shing-Hu, for whom your parents are imprisoned these days?'

It seemed Jigme had thrown molten lead into her ears. Loye writhed in agitation hearing the name of Shyu-Shing-Hu. Her younger brother Sonam had come hastily from Fun-Do yesterday-noon itself.

'Sister! the police have arrested mama and father.'

He wept bitterly. Loye's heart seemed to shrink out of fear. Nobody was in the house at that time. Mother-in-law had gone to a neighbour's house and Jigme was working in the field along with his brothers.

'Why, what happened?'

Pushing strongly to her brother Sonam, Loye lamented deeply.

'Sister, that Shyu-Shing-Hu came to our house. He was very angry. He was telling father that you have not done right to separate Loye from me. The result will not be in your favour.'

'O my God! Then?'

Loye held her head in her hands.

Sonam was explaining while sobbing—

'Father said—She is my daughter. I can take any decision about her.'

Loye interrupted—

'Did his mother also come?'

'He said that I had gone to bring my mother so that you can be assured about my pure intention and also about the future of your daughter.'

'His mother had come to our house or not?'

Loye was irritated on Sonam.

'No, she had stayed in his camp.'

'Then, what happened?'

Loye was breathing quickly.

'Both were discussing harshly. He was very much angry. All of sudden father attacked him with a hatchet.'

Sonam started weeping again remembering that scene.

'O God, what you have to do?'

She sat on the floor almost languidly. Next moment she raised her head anyhow and asked with a weary-voice—

'Is Shyu alive?'

'Yes sister. He was carried away to hospital anyhow injured. After sometime the policemen came and arrested mother and father. I was hidden the whole night in the house of neighbour aunt. With morning, I came to you.'

Sonam's nose and face were dark red due to sobbing.

Till evening the news that Jigme's in-laws have been arrested and sent to jail, was spread all over the village Sakya because. They had wounded a Chinese officer.

Loye was strongly shocked when very next day Jigme had taunted her in this regard. She was being hurt all round. So, holding the hands of her younger brother sonam she walked out from her in-law's house in the deep darkness of the night. Towards an uncertain future and indefinite destination. No desire was left to meet even Shyu-Shing-Hu also. She was not able to rescue her parents from the grip of the police. If she could get strong and affectionate support in her in-law's house, even though she could try to defend her parents. But she was a helpless girl and moreover fate had decided something else for her.

Laying on her bed lady monk Dolma who was that sweet girl Loye in the past, rubbed her hand on her hairless head. Small hairs grown up on her shaved head were pinching in her palm like thorns. Loye had worn Cheevar[1] along with her younger brother Sonam and came to India. As soon as her beautiful hair was shaved, it seemed that the burden of Jigme and Shyu also fell down. Only father and mother living in her heart, were remembered very often and her feeling of guilt used to come out in the form of tears from her eyes.

'Maai, Maai! Look, Chhungchi is saying that I can't go to Tibet now.'

Tashi came by running and sat on the bed of Dolma. The lady-monk had come back into the present from her past.

She was silently observing the face of little Tashi.

'Please, do tell Maai! Will I not go back to my parents?'

'you shall go son. Chhungchi is only teasing you.'

Dolma's voice was very weak.

'No, she was saying that as Maai herself has never gone to Tibet, in the same way we shall also not be able to go there.'

The innocent face of Tashi was in deep melancholy.'

---

1. Cheevar- a loose dress of dark red color of Buddhist monks

'No son, it will not happen so. You will certainly go. Now go outside and enjoy your game. Tomorrow Devyani madam will accompany you in the celebration of Losar.'

Lady-monk Dolma wanted loneliness at this time for herself. Body and mind both were wearied.

9

Standing before the chamber of Geshe Jampa Devyani was thinking that if he will refuse to meet her then she might feel humiliated. What this guard will think about her. After repeated insistence he became ready to carry the Bouquet of roses to Geshe Jampa.

'Madam, I shall not say anything to Gela. You please write down your message on a paper and I shall give it to him.'

'Why?' What is the harm in saying simple sentence that Devyani madam wants to meet you sir?'

'Madam, we are insignificant workers of this institution. If once, sir has forbidden to meet anyone, how can I dare to say that you have come to meet him.'

The guard was right in his logic. Once Devyani thought to go back. What is need of giving good wishes of Losar to Geshe Jampa but the next moment she looked at the guard who was gazing at her with confusion. She took out a pen from her bag and wrote, on the card hanging in the centre of the bunch of flowers 'good wishes for Losar- Devyani'. She gave it to the guard and did not write knowingly the intention to meet. If he will like to meet, he may call, otherwise she will go back. The guard went inside with bouquet.

The curtain of the chamber trembled. Devyani's steps stopped suddenly while walking in the lawn. The guard was coming out of chamber.

'Madam, Gela is calling you.'

The guard told her. There was a variegated expression on his face.

'Overlooking him, Devyani entered the chamber.

'Namaskar[1] Gela!'

---

1.   Namaskar-A Hindi word of wishing anyone as 'good-morning.'

She knowingly wished him in her own mother-tongue.

'Namaskar Devyani! how are you?'

He also replied her in the same way.

'I am fine sir. I went to meet Maai Dolma. She had called me. She is sick and told to take the children of the monastery to the celebration of Losar. I thought, I should wish you too for Losar.'

She completed her ideas in many pieces.

'The roses are very beautiful.'

There was a soft smile like roses itself, floating on lips of Geshe Jampa.

'Jee, I have chosen these roses from your very lawn. The gardener was working there and I requested him to make this bouquet of roses.'

Devyani exposed everything with a slight shyness.

'It is pleasant for me that while coming from Maai's room to my chamber, there were good wishes twinkling in your mind for me. Innumerous small moments of good wishes joined together build the prosperous period in the life of a person.'

Gehse Jampa had given a spiritual turn to her thought. Devyani felt satisfied. It was good and in her favour that Geshe Jampa had not taken it as her shallowness.

'Jee, thank you sir, for your beautiful explanation of my emotions.'

She did smile. Her eyes slightly shrank due to the smile. Geshe Jampa watched this peculiarity of her personality silently and liked it.

'Come here, Devyani!'

Turning back, he instructed her.

'Jee?'

She stopped for a moment.

'While giving the good wishes of Losar, we have some customs that should necessarily be followed.'

Talking about his Tibetan customs, he was turning towards a corner in his chamber. Devyani was following him. A powder like parched grain was put into a rectangular wooden pot on the table. In the very middle of that pot, there was a long cake in the shape of arrow and could be seen from a certain distance also. The cake was wide at the bottom and gradually sharpened at the peak. The cake was decorated by colorful flowers and leaves. In front of the wooden pot of parched grain, there were six or seven clay pots in which green plants of wheat were swaying slowly with the wind. She was enchanted.

'Take a little amount of Chhemar[1] from this pot and spring it up.'

Geshe Jampa himself took parched grain snapping with the fingers and told her by springing it up.

'Jee.'

Devyani followed him.

'It is our offerings to God.'

He further explained.

'Really?'

Devyani's curiosity increased.

'Do you recall the hymn that is chanted on this occasion?'

'No Gela, Not complete…..only three lines-

Tashi Delek Funsum Chhok.

Ema Patro Kunkham Sang.

Tendu Deva Thop-par Shog.'

Reciting the lines, she smiled. Geshe Jampa looked at her with appreciation.

'Yes, it is O.K. Only pronunciation must be corrected.'

'Sir, I feel pleasure to see all these things. I want to know something more.'

Her questioning eyes stayed on the face of Geshe Jampa.

'Ask Devyani!'

'What is this and why?'

She indicated towards green plants of wheat in the clay-pot.

---

1. Chhemar – Parched grain.

'Lo-Fud. It is called Lo-Fud. We pray for prosperity for everybody through it.'

His voice was serious.

'And what do you call to this thing put in Chhemar?'

Devyani again indicated towards the cake kept in Chhemar. She had known the meaning of Chhemar?'

'This is called Chep-to. This is also the symbol of our happiness and sacrifices. This pot, in which Chhemar is kept is called Bo in the Tibetan language.'

Geshe Jampa solved all her curiosity at one time.

'Losar is celebrated in every Tibetan family as you people celebrate your festival of Holi. Khab-Se[1]is the essential sweet of Losar and it is distributed among the people like a boon.'

Geshe Jampa sat on his chair and indicated for her to sit too.

'It is very similar to our rituals sir.'

Sitting on the chair Devyani spoke and Geshe Jampa smiled softly.

'You are here for the last three or four years. Have you never participated in Losar?'

'No sir. It was never celebrated in the monastery. The students use to go the Tibetan Research Centre every year. Maai used to go with them. We never got such an opportunity. It was my decision today to come here otherwise I could not know all these pleasing facts.'

Her eyes laughed before her lips.

'Sometimes the heart takes right decisions.'

Geshe Jampa said while pushing his finger on the call-bell.

'Why? Is it wrong maximum time?'

'The nature of heart is unsteady. Undiscriminating and without reasoning, persisting for incoherent things most of the time. In this condition how can any of its decisions be declared right?'

---

1. Khab-Se- A kind of sweet.

Geshe Jampa kept his hands with the support of the back of the chair turning behind and put himself languidly. His fair complexion became reddish. He closed his eyes.

'Will you not agree to this fact that sometimes the heart becomes undiscriminating and without reason because of our strong connections. We don't want to let it be free. As we tie it up more, it runs away in the opposite direction with the same speed. I think, the heart should be left in its normal condition.'

Devyani gave her own logic. Geshe Jampa opened his eyes and watched her.

'Yes Gela?'

That same guard came in hearing the call-bell and asked him.

'Bring tea.'

He ordered. The guard went out bent-headed. Geshe Jampa again started his talk—

'If you have your fixed destination and have to reach there by horse-riding how can you leave the horse free to wander here and there? To move the horse in your pre-decided direction, you have to command it.'

'But sometimes you have to loosen the bridle in order to make horse turn in any particular direction.'

Devyani had put her strong logic. Her heart was not ready to bow-down.

'You have justified my opinion itself. The heart takes the right decision very often.'

An innocent laughter was twinkling on Geshe Jampa's lips. Today, for the first time Devyani was observing him laughing as a child who wins the game.

'How much have you read of the Buddha?'

All of sudden controlling his laughter Geshe Jampa changed the topic.

'Only to teach.'

She replied.

'I'll give you a book. So many untouched events of Buddha's life are depicted in it. You go through this book and give me your reaction.'

He stood up from his chair, moved ahead towards almirah and took out the book from it. He put the book on the table. Tea was there.

'Sir, is it not a paradox of the present time that there are atom-bombs and other weapons all over the world, conflict and disagreement between so many treaties that are being broken or built on one hand, and on the other hand, there is Lord Buddha, his compassion, preaching of love and peace? Both the two ends, the two extremes? The principle of co-existence, co-operation and peace look like a sandy-palace. What do you think?'

Devyani started again, taking sip of tea.

'No Devyani, today or tomorrow, the world must choose one, either war or Buddha's peace. I do believe that the bent of all minds will be towards peace.'

There was a light of hope in his sight.

'But sir, I think there is a similar relation between war and peace as is in between reality and imagination. War is our truth which is seen by naked eyes till today and peace is our imagination that is always wanted for the continued existence of our beautiful earth.'

'For this cry need of peace Buddha preached the value of compassion, so that this imagination may be real. If compassion exists in the heart of everyman, peace will become a reality of human society.'

Geshe Jampa explained. He liked Devyani's rational talk.

'Is it possible sir? For a moment, it can be thought about by a reasonable person, but if every person of the world is not reasonable. Then?'

The short question of Devyani became global.

'This question is serious yet, but not impossible.'

He was optimistic.

'As I understand it sir, generally it is our empty pride or feeling to oblige someone to which we think of our compassion. There is an indirect desire that it will enhance our glory. In my views, this is not the real form of compassion. Compassion is based on the feeling of equality, absolutely different from the feeling of showing sympathy for a poor person.'

'You are absolutely right Devyani. No strange feeling is found in compassion. The feeling of oneness is itself compassion. Once Lord Buddha saw a patient recumbent in his own filth, he washed him and told his monks— if you want to serve me, first look-after this patient.'

Reciting the story Geshe Jampa's eyes were shining.

'Sir, it can be called co-existence and to bring and join the world together with this emotion should be the motto of life. But to know the reality of the world we must keep ourselves aloof. It can be called the stage of meditation, in our Hindu mythology, it is 'Dhyanavastha', when we peep into ourselves like a neutral person. To know, what is life, it is necessary to be aloof from oneself. As a fish can't know too much about the water because its whole life is watery, but a frog living on the shore, too can know what is water.'

'Buddha emphasized this particular issue. Each and every person has their capability to achieve the highest goal of life. For this, he himself must try. Of-course, the way was shown by Buddha. Now it depends on an individual that how long he takes to achieve his goal through his thoughts and deeds.'

Geshe Jampa put his empty cup on the table.

'Sir, here is the reflection of Shrimadbhagavadgeeta's[1] doctrine of action, as we say it Karmvaad. To get liberated from the worldly circle, self-perception and detachment from the result of action is essential there.'

Devyani also put her empty cup on the table.

'No religion refuses the doctrine of action Devyani. Our deeds are not ineffective. If we do something, it will certainly create its

---

1. Shrimadbhagavageeta- A religious Hindi epic popular as 'Geeta'.

result and it is also not necessary that the result of every action can been seen or found till the death of this physical body.'

'Then faith in rebirth is also crystal clear.'

Devyani's voice was like warbling bird. Geshe Jampa smiled.

'The concept of rebirth is not only in Eastern philosophy but it is in Western Philosophy also Devyani. From Plato to Emerson and so many other philosophers have also accepted the principle of action in one way or another way, that the body is destroyed but action is never destroyed.'

'Then, to begin one's religion with criticizing other's religion is not proper. The destination is one. The paths are different. The aim is the same. The medium is also almost the same. Purity of action. If actions are good and pure then attaining the ultimate Aim itself will be good.'

'Again I repeat the same that compassion is the basis of good action.'

Geshe Jampa insisted on his opinion.

'Then, do you believe sir that your compassion will help to attain the goal of millions of Tibetans? And moreover, if the inner self is so awakened that it stays on the feeling of equality, then what is the meaning of the difference of place, time and circumstances? We Indians have believed in Vasudhaiv Kutumbakam[1] for centuries.'

Geshe Jampa got the hint from Devyani.

'See Devyani! some matters are merged with ones existence. Action, meditation and liberation are very near to it and far away too. To observe the flow of a river, it is essential to stand on the bank of it but to feel the coolness of its water, it is also necessary to go down into it. It means for both feelings, the river is an essential object. Tibet is not only a piece of land for us but it's like a river for these two types of feelings.'

'The same thing I wanted to say sir that now it has become necessary to come down into the water of the river. Standing far

---

1. Vashudhaiv Kutumbakem-Faith in one global family.

away from it, one can only observe the flow of the river. To divert its direction one has to stand in its current firmly like a strong rock. This is not only my opinion but of millions of Indians who believe so.'

Geshe Jampa observed, there was no superficial expression on her face. She had put her opinion before him with complete simplicity. The feeling of officer and subordinate had also disappeared, and in place of that the rational persons of two different countries were sitting before each other. Geshe Jampa smiled softly and said—

'Devyani, let me finish my talk by telling you a Zen story. I don't know, how you will like it, but I myself appreciate it. There was a saint named Rayokan. He used to do his meditation in his small cottage situated in a valley under the hill. A thief came into his cottage one night but there was nothing to be stolen. Rayokan made him stop and said— you came from so distant a place to meet me. It is not proper that you go back empty-handed. You take my clothes as a gift.'

The thief was surprised and went with his clothes. Rayokan still sat in his place and observed the beautiful moon in a mood of bliss. Then, he whispered—Poor man! If it was possible, I could give him this beautiful moon. So Devyani, there are some such things that can't be given to others. The motherland is the same thing.'

Concluding his talk Geshe Jampa stood up. A constant smile was floating on his face. Devyani also stood up from her chair. She took her leave— 'Sir, Thank you for giving me so much time today. I did not expect even to meet you.' Her hands were folded in honour and respect.

'At present, I have only this book to give you.'

Geshe Jampa offered the book to Devyani.

She took it in her hands.

'This is a very precious thing for me sir, No need of moon.'

She laughed softly. Geshe Jampa felt the softness of her laughter silently for a moment and then moved ahead to come out from the room. Devyani also followed him.

10

Returning from the festival of Losar, Devyani handed over the children to Maai Dolma and moved towards her house by rickshaw. It was the beginning of night but the roads had been empty and without noise due to the cold season. This was also the reason that she made up her mind to come out halfway through the programme. Once, when she stood up to come out, Mr. Gyaso, the warden of the hostel, insisted that she should stay more—

'Why are you going just now madam? Will you not listen to my song?'

'Oh yes, why not? I did not know that you sing also.'

She sat again out of courtesy. Mr. Gyaso laughed.

'I don't sing but certainly try to hum today, this very day.'

'You also sing the songs from Hindi films?'

Devyani asked with curiosity because before it so many Tibetan girls and boys had recited the popular songs of Hindi Cinema from the dais.

'Yes, yes, because where can we find Tibetan cinema to sing its song? Moreover, living in India, we like Hindi.'

Mr. Gyaso stood up. The announcer was calling his name from the stage.

'Best of luck, Mr. Gyaso.'

Devyani gave her best wishes to Gyaso and smiled. He accepted it by swaying his hand to the wind and proceeded towards dais.

Devyani started supervising the surroundings at the enclosure erected for this public gathering. There was arrangement for refreshment on the left side of it. Plates and tumblers were kept beautifully. There was a group of Tibetan ladies and gents who were playing cards sitting on the carpet in one corner. Some were sitting together in the cluster of shrubs and were enjoying the dance and music.

Most of the chairs were filled with Tibetan children and young boys. The children who had come with Devyani were also sitting on these chairs. Most of the Tibetan girls had the modern dress like jeans and shirts but a few of them were in their traditional Tibetan dress also. On the right side of the stage there was a horrible faced cut-out made of thick paper with whom the children were playing the game of archery. In the very centre of the Pandal[1] there was a big 'Bo' in which'Chhemar' and 'Chepto' were beautifully kept. There were Lo-Fud also swaying in clay pots, that had been put nearby. Yesterday, Devyani had seen these things in the chamber of Geshe Jampa too.

Mr. Gyaso was singing a romantic song from the dais. The public was encouraging him by clapping at every line. Without any accompanist, the atmosphere was full of merriment. The difference between junior and senior was dissolved there. Devyani observed everything with enchantment. Her mind was filled with a peculiar kind of pleasure.

'Now, I request, my Devyani madam, who is very much here on the eve of this Telo-year, that enjoying our happiness together she also must recite something on this occasion. We are thankful today that she had come to participate in our festival of Losar, this year. Devyani madam, please.'

Concluding his song Mr. Gyaso had called Devyani's name from the stage. Devyani was astonished. Everybody began to look at her with curiosity. She moved ahead towards stage in hesitation. She was unable to understand, what she should recite? The videographer had diverted his camera's focus towards her. The small drops of sweat glittered on her forehead in the sharp light of the sun-gun. She wiped her forehead with the edge of her Saree and asked the cameraman not to take more pictures—

'No please.....'

---

1. Pandal- an enclosure erected for public meeting.

Mr. Gyaso was coming down from the stage. When he saw Devyani asking the cameraman to stop, he whispered slowly coming near to her—

'It is necessary madam. We preserve this Video-recording, so that, whenever needed, we can show that this celebration or gathering was not political.'

Devyani was astonished again. Gyaso continued his dialogue while going towards stage with her.

'Our higher committee of Tibetan officers of this place watch this video-recording whenever needed. The director of our institute, senior Lama of the Tibetan temple, your Geshe Jampa, all.....'

She felt shy when he said 'your Geshe Jampa' but the next moment she understood that Gyaso had no ill intention behind it. It seemed that Gyaso wanted to remain for more time in front of camera in her presence. Devyani did smile.

After reaching on the stage Devyani took the mike in her hand and giving best wishes for Losar to everybody she started singing softly the lines of a Hindi poem-

Apni bhoo par panv tike hon,
Ho apna aakash khula,
Bas mera mujhako mil jaaye,
Chhahun jag se kya aur bhala!

There was a pin-drop silence in the meeting. Everybody was listening to her with deep enchantment. Apart from the film-song, the lines of poetry filled with soft feeling, and words were falling off like the flowers of the coral tree. There spread out an unbreakable silence for a moment.

'Madam, should I turn right or left?'

The rickshaw puller was asking. Devyani stopped reminiscing. She was reminded of Losar again. Her house was near.

'Please uncle, turn right. That house,..... that in the corner.... only in front of that.'

She indicated to him with her index finger and opened her bag to draw the money for payment.

Entering her first room, she stayed a while. She was astonished for a moment that perhaps she had come somewhere else. On the front bed a gentleman, wearing white 'Kurta' and trouser, was half recumbent taking support of a large stuffed pillow. Two other persons, sitting on the chairs beside the bed, were busy in some discussion. Devyani guessed that Mama had welcomed them because the empty cups of tea were kept on the table.

She became worried for a moment. If Deepesh had not been in the house, how Mama could have managed all these?

'You have come Devyani?'

Uncle Suryaprakash was asking her coming out from next room. Deepesh was behind him.

'Sirrah! Uncle you?'

She expressed her happiness and touched his feet.

'Come, let me introduce with everybody. He is the M.L.A. of our area. Now-a-days, he is holding an important position in the ruling party.'

Uncle had introduced that half incumbent person in a flattering manner. Devyani folded her hands to wish him formally. In return the Mr. M.L.A. smiled with curved lips. His face became painted with false pride. A lusty thirst was floating in his eyes for Devyani.

'I should bring tea etc....'

She turned back at once without completing introduction with other two persons. She did not like the arrival of these persons without prior information. She could not imagine by the car standing outside the house that there will be these persons.

'No, No, we have taken everything. Come, and please sit here. We shall talk to you two minutes only and then say goodbye.'

When Mr. M.L.A. spoke to her nonchalantly, she felt a little insulted but composing herself she sat on a chair. Giving her bag to Deepesh, she made Mr. M.L.A. realize her seriousness and position.

'Deepesh! Keep it on my table and tell Mama that I have come.'

'Why have you come so late today Devyani?'

Suryaprakash uncle asked in such a manner as if he was questioning Devyani about her behaviour. Devyani raised her eyebrows in defiance. She did not like to be asked in this way.

Moreover, she was so distressed by the previous behaviour of her uncle that she always used to feel the smell of conspiracy in his normal discourse also. She replied abruptly—

'Now, if a job is there, being late or earlier is quite natural. Sometimes work is less and sometimes much more.'

Suryaprakash uncle did not expect such a rough and abrupt answer from her. He felt insulted.

Mr. M.L.A. put his opinion—

'Above all, it is very hard for women to work outside. The poor ladies are always in trouble to make a balance between house and office.'

'Why, why is it hard?' they adjust easily in both places.'

Devyani became somewhat polite. M.L.A. saheb was encouraged—

'Where do you teach?' He asked.

'Here, very much here in Sarnath….there is an institution. In that very institution I teach Tibetan children.'

She replied in short.

The curiosity of M.L.A. saheb was raised more. He sat carefully. Rubbing the sleeve of his 'Kurta' he asked again—

'In Tibetan language or in Hindi?'

'Jee, both, I know both languages.'

'Very good. How many students are there?'

He was being more curious.

'Their numbers differ in every institute. Moreover, they are millions in number all over India.'

Devyani gave a fuzzy data.

'Look! the population of our country is already increasing day and night and above all, the Government has to spend on them too.'

M.L.A. saheb showed his worries for country.

'You people never raised their problem as an electoral subject. How can the problem be removed. If the population of our country is increasing, it is also due to the policy of appeasement. Some are free in the name of religion, some are singing their own song of minority and increasing the population day and night so that they can establish their vigour all over the world. our leaders are always busy in capturing the ruling chairs by hook or by crook, keeping aside all these national problems. Only their business is limited in pulling the leg of the opposite party. Why shouldn't the country's future be in question? '

Devyani protested.

'Oh, you are giving a speech like the leader of the opposition party madam.'

M.L.A. saheb laughed. The thirst in his eyes deepened. The rest of the people were gazing at Devyani constantly. There was an expression of surprise on their faces. The feeling of how a lady can argue with a leader, was coming and going on their faces.

'When my elder brother, means Devyani's father was alive, he used to say that he would make Devyani a leader. She is very intelligent. She has been logical from her very childhood.'

Uncle Suryaprakash had changed the topic. Remembering her father Devyani again filled with bitterness for her uncle. How he deceived her father. Uncle had encroached the whole paternal land just after the death of her grandfather putting his single name on the documents. Living most of the time outside from the village due to his service, her father could not guess his younger brothers deviousness. After his retirement, when he returned to live in the village, then elder persons of the village made him understand. Father had tolerated somehow but in the eyes of Mama and Devyani, uncle could never be worthy of forgiveness.

'I should prepare a meal for you people.'

She tried for leave.

'No, no need of a meal at all, I wanted to meet you, that has been done. Now I shall proceed. My car is there. I shall reach my destination within two hours.'

M.L.A. saheb sat consciously.

Uncle further said—

'Devyani, you can remember that petrol pump, 'Radhe Service', that is on the way from our village to Varanasi, that petrol pump belongs to M.L.A. saheb. Radhekant is his younger brother and hence his name is there. He looks after it. He is unmarried yet.'

Devyani's sixth sense became conscious. She thought, perhaps uncle has again come with some marriage proposal.

'No lady in my family is in a job. Service means dependence on others. Who goes to become 'yesman' of someone in service, and for ladies, it is totally impossible. The question does not arise.'

M.L.A. saheb gave a hint and Devyani received the whole matter. She replied with a cool temper—

'Yes, you are absolutely right. Ladies of the same mentality are also needed in your family otherwise it will be very difficult to lead the family. There are so many ladies too who do not like to do service, or go outside the house.'

Telling it she laughed tauntingly.

M.L.A. saheb felt perplexed for a moment and the next moment he changed the topic— 'No, I am in favour of it that the nature of family must change now.'

'But first of all, the gents of your family should start seeking and doing jobs, after that ladies' jobs will look proper, otherwise inferiority complex will be developed between them.'

'Yes, yes, you are right. Now, let us move.'

Standing from his chair. M.L.A. saheb said. His face reflected restlessness now.

'One minute, I am just coming meeting my Bhabhi.[1]'

Uncle insisted M.L.A. to stay for a while more, indicating Devyani to come inside, he entered the next room.

Devyani also came behind him. Entering the next room uncle showed his annoyance with Devyani.

---

1. Bhabhi-Elder brother' wife.

'This family is so reputed and rich and you were giving a speech like Laxmibai[1] before them. Why?'

'You should have asked me first uncle. Why did you come straight here with them.?'

Devyani also replied in the same way.

'Lo! Look Bhabhi, after passing away of my elder brother, I did want to fulfill my responsibility by making these children settled, so that none can tell me that after their father's death, uncle also left them helpless, the daughter of my elder brother remained unmarried and this girl?' she is arguing with me. Now you see yourself. I hold my ears at this very moment that I'll intervene in this matter. This was a prosperous family that is why I thought about this relation. What is kept in your service of six or seven thousand rupees that you are kicking aside such a wealthy family?'

Uncle was angry.

'If my thoughts do not match with that family, what will I do by going in that family?' Devyani again defeated him with her logic.

'Lo, again! Will you tally your thoughts first, then marry?'

Uncle tapped his forehead. Devyani could not like his irrational talk— 'Uncle, every word has several meanings. Don't twist my sentence in this way.'

'Yes, yes I am not so intelligent as you people are. Please excuse me. It was my fault that I thought for this marriage by considering you my own Kith and Kin.'

Uncle told. Mama reacted in a slow voice—

'No. Bhaia, we also are not considering you different from us. Only, you should have talked before hand.

All of a sudden, one should not exhibit his daughter before some alien person.'

'Now, please, you people excuse my fault. I go.'

And uncle went out in anger. Deepesh also went behind him to see him off.

---

1. Laxmibai-A brave freedom fighter of India.

11

'May I come in sir?'

Removing the curtain of Geshe Jampa's chamber aside, Devyani asked. Today, as she came to the institute the guard had informed her—

'Madam, sir has called you.'

'Why? Is anything important?'

She was astonished.

'I don't know madam, only he has said to send you as soon as you come.'

The guard informed her. Going towards her classroom, Devyani turned to Geshe Jampa's chamber.

'Yes, come in Devyani.'

Geshe Jampa called her by reading a paper with bowed head.

'Jee, Tashi Delek sir.'

Reaching near his table Devyani wished him in a quiet voice. Geshe Jampa raised his head once, saw Devyani and indicated her to sit. Devyani felt as if he was worried today. There was yellowish light spread out in the chamber at during day time also. The thick curtains on the window and doors were swaying slowly and filtered light coming through these curtains was not enough that one could read anything easily in it. Perhaps this was the reason that Geshe Jampa lit the table lamp also. In the golden light of the lamp his fair complexion became more golden. Today he had worn the orange colour 'Cheevar' and it enhanced his glory. On his right wrist, there was a sandal-chaplet surrounding it.

'One minute Devyani, I will talk to you in a minute.'

He gave a hint by right hand and again became busy in reading.

'Don't worry sir, I am sitting.'

Devyani said politely and diverted her eyes towards the paintings hanging on the walls of chamber but after few moments her attention was again drawn towards Geshe Jampa. The small black mark was shining on his chest just below the throat. The wide shoulder and arms were opened as usual and the muscles of his arms were trembling very slowly. Keeping his right palm under his chin, he was thinking something. Devyani forcibly removed her eyes from him.

'What is the matter Gela? Is anything new?'

Asking him, the lady-monk Dolma also had entered the chamber.

'Come Maai! take your seat.'

Geshe Jampa welcomed her, and Devyani stood-up in her place.

'Oh, Devyani madam you?'

Dolma was surprised to see Devyani in Geshe Jampa's chamber. Devyani also became hesitant for some time. Before Devyani could reply, Geshe Jampa made it clear why he had called then—

'I have called both of you. Actually I have to go outside from this city for some essential work.'

'Where?'

Dolma asked sitting on the chair. Devyani also sat silently.

'I have to go to Dharmshala. A letter has come from there.'

He was looking towards them now.

'Is anything serious Gela?'

The lady-monk was curious.

'Yes, certainly will be. It will be clear after going there. At present I have been informed only that there is an emergency meeting of Kashag.[1] The senior officers from Geneva and Kembra offices are also coming to participate in it.'

Geshe Jampa was serious.

'This Kashag is of your exiled Government sir?'

Devyani could not control her curiosity.

---

1. Kashag-Tibetan name for parliament of their exiled government.

'Yes, and I myself a small worker of it.'

He smiled. Devyani also gave a silent reply by her smile and asked her next question—

'What is the base of Kashag? I mean the process of election?'

'Completely democratic. For five years. His Holiness the Dalai Lama is its president.'

'Where is its head-quarters?'

When Devyani asked this question, Geshe Jampa became serious.

'For the time being, it is in Kangra, Dharmshala, Himachal Pradesh in India. There are so many international offices also in different countries like Switzerland, New York, Nepal, Japan, Australia, France….and many others….'

'When do you meet these officers generally?'

Devyani asked but next moment she understood that it was a complicated question. But Geshe Jampa made it clear.

'We call our meetings whenever we have to think on a serious issue. It is not necessary that all the officers may gather in the same or every meeting. For example this time the officers from Kembra of Australia and Geneva of Switzerland are coming to participate in this meeting. I have met with the officer of Geneva previously but the officer of Kembra is totally new for me. I shall meet him for the first time after the election.'

Geshe Jampa satisfied Devyani with his answer.

'Will this very form of the Government be in future also, when Tibet is liberated?'

The next question of Devyani was really complicated but Geshe Jampa tried to make it clear too—

'Actually Devyani, His Holiness the Dalai Lama has a different idea for the formation of the government of free Tibet. He wants to see a single house parliament and in the house, there must be the complete representation of the public. To form any law, the majority of the house will be essential. The election should be based on the adult public vote cast including monks also. Including all these points he has planned to form his internal constitution, that is certainly different from the ancient half-feudalistic theory and are indication of a new arrangement. Nobody will object to it, I do believe so because it is a demand of the present time.'

'I wish you good luck sir that your dream may be fulfilled.'

Devyani wished him with a smile.

'Thanks Devyani. Dreams, also need some support and that support of our dream is you people. Your love, co-operation and sacrifices itself are our reinforcement.'

Geshe Jampa's eyes stayed on Devyani. There was an undulating ocean in his eyes mingled with love and gratitude. Devyani stopped herself from sinking in it by bowing down her eyelashes.

'Maai, in this one week you will be the guardian of this institution and monastery too. Devyani will be with you. You can contact me by telephone, if you feel any trouble.'

Geshe Jampa's fingers were playing with a paper-weight.

'O.K. Gela! Don't worry.'

Maai Dalma assured him.

'Above all, I have told my senior clerk also to be in contact with you both. Devyani, have you any problem?'

Geshe Jampa asked Devyani again.

'No sir, no problem. Any other assignment if you want to give....'

'It is not my order. I am taking your support. Sometimes one's heart begins to have faith in someone unknowingly. I too feel that I can be mentally free by giving you some responsibility. Only for this reason.....'

Geshe Jampa became emotional but suddenly it was hidden behind his seriousness.

'Jee, it is my luck and pleasure too.'

Devyani could say only these few words out of hesitation.

'You are right Gela. I also like Devyani very much. Very responsible. The children all seem to be mad about Devyani madam. She can make them dance like monkeys. They all are very obedient to her. I think, Devyani knows some magic.'

Maai Dolma was supporting Geshe Jampa with a free laughter and Devyani was smiling only watching Maai Dolma. She felt very embarrassed hearing her own appreciation.

Geshe Jampa felt her hesitation.

Don't disclose my tour unless it is very necessary.'

'Yes sir, I got the point.'

Devyani replied. Her hesitation vanished.

'You don't have the telephone number of that place Devyani. Keep this number with you. Whenever you need, you can dial me.'

Writing the telephone number on a paper Geshe Jampa gave it to Devyani.

'Can your journey be extended more than a week sir?'

She took the paper from his hand and asked. The soft touch of Geshe Jampa's finger awakened a kind of soft sensation in her. There was a shadow of deviation on the face of Geshe Jampa too, that Devyani observed, but the next moment it disappeared.

'It may be extended, it may not be. I shall let you know.'

Geshe Jampa pretended to be normal hiding his emotions in his heart that were restless to show themselves on his face.

'You are going tomorrow morning Gela?'

Lady-monk Dolma asked standing up from her chair.

'Yes.' He also stood up.

Devyani had stood up before him.

'Be watchful about the activities of the institute Devyani.'

Moving ahead towards door, he made her alert once again.

'O.K. sir. Have confidence in me.'

She folded her hands to say goodbye to him. Geshe Jampa accepted her wish with a smile and turned toward his chair.

His chamber filled with an unbreakable silence. He remained feeling it unwittingly for sometime and then engaged himself in his files.

12

'We were hungry and thirsty too but walked together the whole night. Sonam's and my legs became injured with stumbling many times. The lips used to become dry again and again and their skin formed crusts, which were softened only by the wetness of our tongues. But this relief was momentary. No road was also there. Holding each other's hand, we were wandering on the narrow and stony by-path track. There was no sign of life for a long distance.

'Aachaa, I feel fear.'

'Sonam's voice was trembling out of fear. I myself too was frightened but by being elder I could not express it otherwise he might be more frightened. I wanted to rescue myself by coming out of the village Sakya as soon as possible so that they may not find even my shadow. Early in the morning a dog barked and a house also was seen at some distance. A lamp kindled in our sinking hearts.'

Sitting on the rickshaw with Devyani, Maai Dolma was reciting her past story. The pictures of the past were brought alive for a moment and vanished gradually in her mind.

'how many years Lama Sonam Dakpa is younger to you?'

Devyani asked Maai Dolma.

'Completely six years younger....but now he is tired and looks old, tolerating his mental agony since childhood.'

The lady monk wiped her tears in Cheevar. Since Devyani had told her about the serious sickness of her house-owner, since that time Maai Dolma had revived her and Sonam Dakpa's past in many pieces. Many times the ocean of tears had broken its limit. Devyani became very happy when she came to know that Lama Sonam Dapka was the real younger brother of Maai Dolma.

'I'll go with you tomorrow Devyani. I shall come back after seeing him.'

When Maai said this, Devyani could not control her curiosity.

'Maai, I have never seen you talking about your brother or your curiosity to meet him so much.....'

Devyani left her sentence incomplete.

'Devyani, now the delusion from which to get rid of, I became a monk when I was very young, why should I be tied up with the same infatuation. It gives grief.'

Devyani guessed, the hidden emotions behind the rational answer of Maai Dolma.

'Do you not feel sorry to hear about him or being not hearing about....'

Devyani asked and lady monk became wordless for a moment.

'The message of Buddha's compassion can inspire you to consider everyone as one's own but I think, it is impossible indeed, to make aliens of our own blood-relations.'

Devyani gave her logic again.

'Perhaps you are right Devyani.'

And the very next day Maai Dolma moved with Devyani to see her brother Sonam Dakpa.

'When you saw a house early in the morning, then what did you do?'

Devyani wanted to know Maai Dolma's past. She started again.

'The same house-owner had helped us. We told him everything that was true with us. He became kind to us. Without caring of any danger he gave us shelter for two days in his house. The third day that deiform gentleman arranged to send us to India by giving a lot of food and a mule to ride, so that we could reach the border of India safely. Passing through the roadless and untraversable paths amidst the hills of south-eastern Bhutan we could enter India. Before crossing the Pang-po river, we had to cross a cleft between the hills named 'Chela'. The way to it was rough and tiring.I tremble till today when I remember that scene of how we reached in the plains of the river after descending and ascending three or four hours. Miseries never come alone. There was a storm as we came to the plain. We had never seen such a storm earlier in our life. A storm that could make a person blind. We sat on the ground holding each other tightly. Perhaps, it was the last storm of our life in Tibet. We got a kind of peace and assurance as we reached India. It seemed that we had found our father's lap.'

Maai Dolma's eyes were filled with tears out of the emotion of recalling her past.

'Had you taken it otherwise when Lama Sonam Dapka accepted family life after living his long monk-life?'

Devyani suddenly asked. Dolma saw her seriously first and then replied—

'It was pleasant and unpleasant both.'

'Why?'

'Because he had destroyed his austerity of so many years. To become a monk is a symbol of good luck to a man in our society, Devyani. But I felt good for this reason that he supported such a helpless lady who could be broken for lack of shelter. Here, Sonam's compassion is proper in my eyes.'

'There is no scope of proper or improper in compassion, if it is true.'

'Yes, your opinion is also right.'

'Come Maai! come down! Be careful....'

Devyani helped Dolma to come down from the rickshaw by giving support to her in front of her house. They had reached home.

'Lamaji, see, who has come with me?'

Devyani called reaching before the door and Lobjang came out hearing her voice.

'Sirrah! Aachaa you?'

Lobjang did bloom out of joy.

'Who is there?'

The weak voice of Lama Sonam Dakpa came out from inside the room.

'Aachaa is here Lamaji! Aachaa Loye! she has come with Devyani Madam.'

Lobjang moved towards the room giving support to Dolma with her hands.

'Aachaa, Tashi Delek!'

Lama Sonam Dakpa tried to rise from the bed.

'Please, you take rest Lamaji, Doctor has forbidden you to rise from the bed….Aachaa, you please sit here.'

Lobjang told Together.

Devyani was watching silently the ebb and flow of Sonam Dakpa's face. He was trying to control his emotions forcibly. His lips were trembling. It seemed that he would weep bitterly before his sister. The same condition was with Maai Dolma also. She sat on the corner of her brother's bed and silently caught his hands in her own hand stroking it softly. Her eyes were full of tears. Attachment was superseding the detachment.

'Devyani, come for a while.'

Devyani's mother called her from her room.

'Maai! I just come, listening to my Mama.'

Devyani took permission.

'O.K. Devyani! Please take me back to the monastery before it is evening.'

The lady-monk's voice was full of emotion.

'Aachaa, please stay with us today.'

Lobjang requested Dolma.

'No Lobjang, I can't stay. The children are alone in monastery.'

Dolma wiped her tears hiding them from the others.

'What is the matter Mama?'

Devyani asked her mother who was standing at the door.

'Come here?'

Mother turned towards inside the room.

'Where is Deepesh?'

Coming inside Devyani asked.

'In the next room.'

Mother sat on a stool.

'A boy had come some time ago and informed Deepesh that Pema and his friends are arrested and kept in police station.'

Mother told her.

'Why? What is the matter?'

There was a feeling of surprise and fear both on Devyani's face.

'He was taking drugs, perhaps brown sugar in the ruins of Sarnath with his friends. The police-inspector had caught him red-handed.'

'Then, it is a very serious thing Mama.'

Devyani murmured—

'Not only serious, if the police-inspector will put the serious charges upon him, then he will go away forever.'

Deepesh came and stood beside her.

'Lamaji knows or not?'

Devyani asked.

'I have told Lobjang alone. She herself has forbidden me to let Lamaji know otherwise he will be more ill. Poor lady.....she was weeping abusing her fate. Telling— how I have brought them up by doing labour and small jobs but they are not ready to feel my sacrifices.... What a pitiable time has come. The same story is in every house...it is here in India or in Rangoon, tears and laughter are pre-decided in one's destiny. Poor Lobjang... She is already worried for her husband and now the worthy son has given another shock.....hunh.'

Mother was babbling and Devyani was worried. By living in the same house, the problem of that family also seemed to be her own.

'I have called you for this very purpose that do not talk about Pema before Lamaji. Lobjang has told him that Pema has gone to Delhi in search of some job.'

Mother had made Devyani to understand. The lines of worries increased on her face. Lamaji was sick and in this condition she has to help Lobjang anyhow on humanitarian ground, while

Devyani's nature was to keep herself aloof from the police and police-stations.

'Deepesh, go and try to know the possibilities of their getting rid of the charges. Now, we have to tolerate all these problems too if we are living in their house.'

To escape from the argument of Deepesh, Devyani told everything at a time.

'But let Lobjang also say something Didi. She has not uttered a single word and you agreed for bail of Pema.'

Deepesh was irritated.

'What do you think that she will not ask for support? When Maai Dolma will go, she will certainly ask. She does not want to disclose anything before Maai Dolma….poor lady.'

Devyani took favour of Lobjang.

'No Devyani Madam, don't think to rescue Pema at all. Let him rest in jail. He has made my life hell. Sometimes hitting and sometimes merry making only…. I manage bread and butter for them by sucking my own blood and he used to throw dust in my eyes till today. He was telling me— I am learning computer. I also believed, and thought that after learning computer he will be engaged in a job, and life will be settled but he always deceived me. He cheated my breast-feeding. I wanted to make him join Tibetan police-force but my all dreams have been destroyed. Don't get him released. Let him taste the fruit of his own evil deeds.'

Standing behind Devyani Lobjang sobbed. Her nose and eyes were red. She could not stop herself by coming behind Devyani.

'Don't weep Lobjang. We are with you. Give him one chance to correct himself. Perhaps he can adopt the right path.'

Devyani tapped on Lobjang's shoulders with her hands affectionately.

'No Devyani Madam, he will not correct himself. I have already tried many times hiding it from Lamaji. It is not his first chance, earlier also he had committed such a blunder and I tried to reform him but there was no effect on him.'

Lobjang was wiping her tears in her scarf.

'One request is there Devyani Madam, please don't disclose this incident before Lamaji or Aachaa Loye at all, otherwise…'

'Before your direction, my Mama has already told this fact to me. You don't worry.'

Devyani assured Lobjang again.

'Come Devyani Madam, Aachaa Loye was remembering you. I came here to call you.'

Lobjang turned back. Devyani observed that the Chhupa[1]of Lobjang was torn at many places. The sleeve of her blouse also was torn on one place.

'You don't worry Sonam. I am with you. This amulet is made by my senior Lamaji. You wear it on your arm and everything will be alright within a few days.'

Entering the room of Sonam Dakpa with Lobjang Devyani saw that lady monk Dolma was tieing an amulet with white thread on the arm of Sonam Dakpa.

'Yes Lamaji, now it has been sure that everything will be alright. There is blessing of your elder sister too with this amulet, so it will give its positive results much more and very soon.'

Devyani tried to boost up the morale of Lamaji. She was aware of the fact that many irremediable diseases also are cured by strong will power and sometimes very small problems also take the form of incurable disease out of depression.

'Where has Pema gone Lobjang? He might have dropped me off at the monastery. Why must I bother Devyani madam?'

The lady monk had a glance everywhere in search of Pema.

'What botheration Maai! I shall drop you or Deepesh will go with you. Perhaps Pema has gone to Delhi for some personal reasons, isn't that so Lobjangji?'

Devyani tried to handle the situation.

'No madam, he will not be gone anywhere. He might be engaged in loitering somewhere. He knows that I am bed-ridden

---

1. Chhupa- A Tibetan dress.

and Lobjang is busy in managing bread and butter. He has nothing to do with household problems of day to day life….his only younger brother Dava…….he never cares for him also. Dava comes alone on the road from his school daily…. a small child… there are so many cars and vehicles coming and going with speed. If something happens any day then…'

Lama Sonam Dakpa wheezed while speaking.

'Please you keep quite Lamaji. Doctor has forbidden you to speak. Everything will be alright. Everything will be…'

Lobjang started to rub his chest.

'Should I keep Dava with me in the monastery?'

Maai Dolma put her proposal hearing his problem.

'The problems will not be finished only by removing Dava. If he remains with me, sometimes I can come here to give Lamaji his medicine etc. and he watches the shop. It will be more difficult for me if he goes.'

Lobjang's voice was pitiable.

'I shall take him to the institute with me daily and come back too. Now, Lamaji, your one problem has been finished. You live without tension and get well soon.'

Devyani made the atmosphere light by her laughter.

'You support us too much Devyani madam.'

Saying this Lamaji closed his eyes. The lady-monk Dolma was constantly observing her brother's face. Many waves of affection were coming and going on her face.

13

The meeting of Kashag was going on. All of the officers had taken their seats. The hall was filled with the smell of fresh flowers. Bottles of water and tumblers covered with plates were kept before each officer. The shining tables were kept in a 'U' shape in the hall and a big flower-pot decorated with different kinds of flowers was in the centre of the empty space. Beautiful lighting near several huge paintings hanging on the walls were captivating the attention of everybody. The portrait of Buddha in traditional Tibetan style and the flag of the exiled government of Tibet was put at the entrance of the hall on a table. Books in the Tibetan language and others were well decorated in the almirahs of glass kept beside the right wall of the hall. The white and auburn coloured imported pet rats, looking like rabbits were running here and there on the carpet.

The chair person was addressing the officers—

'The condition of Tibet is getting pitiable day by day. Now there are attacks going on its religious traditions too along with the exploitation of social, economic and political issues. The children are forced to learn the Chinese Language 'Mandarin' in the schools, so that our language and identification can be destroyed. They are doing it in the name of development. The numbers of monks in Tibetan monasteries and Temples has been lessened. Where there used to be eight thousand monks in each monastery, now their number has been lessened and you can count them on your fingers. There is restriction on religious preaching.

The action of China about Panchen Lama is also very surprising and contradictory. Surprising for this reason that now China also stated to have faith in Incarnationism and Rebirth and contradictory to it China itself is violating that agreement under which Tibet had been given religious freedom. He says that in selection of Panchen Lama the necessary rituals were not completed, so the Panchen accepted by His Holiness the Dalai Lama is false, while the whole world knows that from the death of the Panchen Lama to the search of a new Panchen, Tibetans have their own customs and traditions. The final decision on it is taken by His Holiness because he is our president along with being our guide and religious-teacher of Tibetans. There has been a commotion in Tibet as China has appointed its own new Panchen Lama. The situation became so bad in Tibet that the administration had to enforce a curfew. No doubt this turmoil is an indication of the raising voice of freedom in Tibet.

But today, the problems to which we want to draw your attention, this meeting has been called is related to two serious points. First, the Tibetan hostiles who are our own people but being trained against us and second, some misguided people in our exiled democratic government. This is unfortunate news also but not confirmed yet that a hit list of Tibetan public leaders had been issued to kill them and in this organization some of our Tibetan people are involved. The security forces have arrested some youngsters in these very early days. These youngsters are given allurement to do such heinous crimes. The investigation is going on. We have to think on this issue too, how the feeling of nationalism must be filled in the hearts of those who are living far away from us because, this misguided young generation is born in the present time and who has not seen our past or the miseries of 1959. No media or literature can reach straight forward to them. So, we have to think about them in a new dimension.

On the other hand, wherever, we people are residing as refugees, there we are training our young boys and girls to save their culture and vanity. Constantly we are involved in reviving the Buddha religion, Tibetan culture, history, astrology and medicines here in India without any fear. The translations, editing and literary-creations are going on without interruption, but some Tibetan people are confused under the influence of western culture. Our emphasis should be on this topic also today that how they can be reformed and involved with the main aim.

The most reckoning thing is this that a confidential report of all our activities in every country is sent to China. Whenever any Tibetan person becomes active for his Mukti-Sadhna,[1] he is called back to Tibet on the ground of some emotional pretension and when he reaches there, all his activities are done finished. If they are unable to break his will power, they don't hesitate to finish that very person. Thus our goal weakens. A moral pressure is always with us that our old parents and relatives are there in Tibet in miserable conditions and to call back our active members from other countries, they use them. They are tortured wildly so that they become bound to call them back. Thus on the basis of emotional torture they are making our mission weak.

In this reference I would like to tell you that a few days before, a letter was received by our Kashag, in the name of our Education Minister Geshe Jampa. His father has written this letter....after reading the letter, it is very much clear that he was forced to write this letter....' The sentence of chair person was emotional and somehow broken.

The secret revelation by the chair person in the meeting shocked Geshe Jampa. He became restless hearing about his father. Controlling himself anyhow he bent his head and supported it by his hands but his eyes filled with tears which could not be hidden. The chair person was speaking further—

'I shall provide him the photocopy of that letter, but we must decide our strategy on this issue also, whether we should send back our active members to Tibet on the basis of such emotional blackmailing or not? I wish that Geshe Jampa must keep his view on this particular issue today in this meeting.'

When the chair person spoke, Geshe Jampa stood up in his place and controlling his emotions he replied politely—

---

1. Mukti-Sadhna-Non-violent Tibetan freedom movement.

'Honourable sir, I need some time to say anything in this reference. Above all, whatever will be the decision of the majority in this meeting, I'll perform my duty accordingly.'

Geshe Jampa sat after giving his opinion. He was very serious. Very frequently his father's face was rolling before his eyes. How many times Geshe Jampa wrote letters to his father from India on the address of his home-town but he never received any response. He consoled his heart-perhaps Mama and father are no more in the world. But all of sudden this letter from his father? From where he might have written? Geshe Jampa became restless to hear about the letter. His heart began throbbing for Mama-how will she be? Father will have been very old. Will they recognize their Jampa? How many changes have come between little Jampa and this Geshe Jampa? But Mama will certainly recognize him. Mother' emotions never accept the factors of time and space.

'Now, I invite the opinion of Mr. Chhering Topgyal, the head of our Kembra office.'

When the chair person had called the name of Chhering Topgyal, Geshe Jampa looked there. An aged gentleman started to speak holding the mike in his hand. He was about sixty five or seventy years old.

'I begin with that particular point where our honorable chairman has finished his speech. Whether our active members should be sent to Tibet or not? This particular point is very complicated, but I think, our movement has arrived at its final stage now. We can't go there together. The Tibetan group on the border of India, who were trying to go back to Tibet, but China opposed it before India. It is a clear-cut evidence of it. Every country has its foreign-policy and India has too. We are not in favour of attaining our goal by putting someone else in problems. But it will be better now if we start to go to Tibet one by one with our mission and must organize our people there in order to give a final shape to our movement.

Geshe Jampa is an intelligent and efficient member of our organization and that is why he is given the important charge of education. In my opinion it is a golden chance for him to go to Tibet and to light the lamp of revolution. Gradually all of us make our programme to go to Tibet now. We have almost completed our external mission. The world majority is with us. Africa and American countries are co-operating with us. To be given the highest award of the world, the Nobel Prize for Peace to His Holiness Dalai Lama is the evidence that the whole world has accepted our non-violent freedom movement as a genuine matter. Above all, in China itself there is evolving an unrest internally in favour of democracy. This is a golden opportunity when we can try to organize our own people too. Except some people, the rest of the Tibetans have unbreakable will power today also. Hundreds of public-agitations have taken place in the last decade in which thousands of Tibetans lost their lives. Innumerable Tibetans are kept in prisons about whom no information is given to the public. I am the eye-witness of the agitation of 1959 when near about eighty seven thousand Tibetans were killed brutally and His Holiness was bound to leave Tibet.'

Geshe Jampa again was astonished. He was watching this representative of Kembra named Chhering Topgyal carefully. He was unable to understand, why this face was looking so near and dear to him? When this representative quoted the incident of 1959 at Lhasa, Geshe Jampa was reminded of Mag-pa. He also remembered that incident of how Mag-pa had entered the house in the darkness of night and how Mama had saved him by helping him escape from the back-door. But that black-night had scattered his whole family.

Geshe Jampa again watched very carefully this representative of Kembra who was delivering his lecture. While speaking the trembling big and brown coloured mole beside the ear was visible. Geshe Jampa's heart became unsteady. The same kind of mole was on his Mag-pa's face too that used to tremble while telling him a story. Once little Jampa had touched it and asked—

'Mag-pa, you have three ears.'

Mag-pa laughed loudly and said—

'Yes, so that I can hear the distant voice from far away.'

'Of Aachaa Chinaye also?'

Jampa asked innocently.

'Yes, may be…. if she can really call me once, only once my dear, then….'

Mag-pa became emotional.

Jampa was unable to understand anything. He knew only that his sister Chinaye was lost somewhere.

'Sir, this letter.'

As a peon whispered before him putting a letter on his file. Geshe Jampa suddenly came into present from the past and hastily took that letter in his hand. This was the same letter about which the chair person had spoken just sometime before. Geshe Jampa's attention diverted from Chhering Topagyal and he tried to recognize the writing of this letter. It was just like his father's writing.

He recognized it immediately and the remaining doubts also were removed when he saw written as, 'Thupten' at the end of the letter. His eyes again filled with tears. His emotions were out of control. Without reading the letter, he stroked it softly with his palm as if he was touching his father's hand. the soft and gentle words like delicate green grass started to tell their story themselves raising their heads—

Lhasa

Telo

18th April

My heart Jampa,

Love!

How I spent so many years, I can't write. Only I shall say son, you come back. Your mother is counting her last days. The tortures in jail and departure of her children has made her life-less. She has lost her memory also. I am so unfortunate a man that I could not escape even from the memories of past life. You set us free from this life of hell my son! The officers here have agreed on this condition also that if you live here peacefully after coming from India and do not take part in anti-national activities, they will release us from the prison and will let us live life peacefully.

I want to spend the rest of my days with you. Perhaps, thus, your mother also can survive a few days more. The lamp of life is on the edge of end. Come back my dear son!

Your father

Thupten

He was reading the letter and on the other hand, Chhering Topagyal was concluding his lecture—

'No doubt there will be a problem in adjustment between exiled Tibetans and the Tibetans who are living in Tibet itself after getting freedom but it is not a difficult task. We are conscious about it also.'

When the meeting finished, Geshe Jampa could not stop himself. Hastily he reached before Chhering Topagyal who was going out from the hall and said—

'My self is Jampa. I came here in my childhood. Nang-gr-che was my native-village. Are you acquainted with that place?'

Chhering Topagyal was shocked suddenly. He watched Geshe Jampa very carefully adjusting his glasses on his eyes, as if he wanted to recognize Jampa. Holding his Cheevar on his shoulder properly, he again looked at Jampa seriously. His thin lips were trembling with the emotions of joy and surprise both. His cheeks full of wrinkles twinkled with a reddish light. Embracing Jampa in his arms he asked—

'Chinaye's brother Jampa?'

'Yes, yes sir, Aachaa Chinaye… she was my sister.…'

Geshe Jampa was looking in his eyes impatiently.

'Oh, Jampa…my Jampa.'

Chhering Topgyal filled him in his arms warmly and embraced him looking towards sky.

Tears started overflowing from their eyes.

'Mag-pa, you are my Mag-pa? Is'nt it?'

Geshe Jampa asked with a choked voice.

'Yes…. yes….' I am your Mag-pa.

They both were unable to speak further. Everybody stayed for a while and started to look at them.

'I am in suit No. 14, you come there in the evening Jampa.'

Chhering Topagyal became conscious about his responsibilities given to him and he affectionately separated Geshe Jampa, giving him instruction to come in the evening. It seemed that someone has rubbed red colour on Jampa's nose and cheek. He wiped his eyes with his palm.

'Yes, I'll come.'

Geshe Jampa controlled himself. Both of them moved towards their rooms with heavy steps.

The sun before setting was shining on the peak of a mountain. The shadows of trees were longer and visible on the plains. The pink lotuses were half-budded in the ponds situated out side the building of the Kashag. The fishes were creating a commotion in the calm water of the pond. There was an unbreakable silence everywhere in the atmosphere.

14

Chhering Topgyal was reciting his past story to Geshe Jampa being half-recumbent on the bed in his room. Geshe Jampa sat beside his leg and was rubbing it softly. Looking at Mag-pa constanly, he was listening to him. He was emotional to find his Mag-pa after such a long gap and feeling as if his childhood had come back and the emotions of Mama and father also entered Mag-pa's soul.

'When I came out from your house on that dark night, at that time hiding myself from the sight of soldiers I met anyhow with the members of my organization early in the morning, wandering on the rugged path. At once we took the decision to leave Tibet immediately otherwise our lives were in danger. In this situation our mission could not proceed further. A griping pain was constantly there in my heart after leaving you people that how had the soldiers behaved with you.'

Mag-pa made his throat clear. Geshe Jampa stood up and gave a tumbler of water to wet his throat. After drinking water Mag-pa again started—

'We went by motor-car near about sixty km. from Lhasa. But further, the roads were under-construction. The construction of these roads was the second cause of unrest in Tibetans. The Tibetan labourers were forced to work on this project for very less payment. We also had to admit till now that these roads are necessary for the development but how these roads were being constructed under the policy of exploitation and suppression that was very painful for all. Anyway, we were moving ahead on those half-constructed roads riding on mules. All the time we were alert, that somewhere, the soldiers could not watch us. All of a sudden the heavy rain made our paths more troublesome but now we were assured somehow that in such bad weather, the soldiers would not like to come out of their camps.

We were moving ahead. Somewhere the foundation of the roads were ruined due to heavy rain. Wherever on these routes we were unable to take support of mules too, we crossed those muddy ways on foot walking with mules. These hillside roads were dangerous too because the heavy rocks from the hills could fall down anytime on our heads, but there was inbilation in our hearts. The soul of your sister was constantly with me. Do you remember the face of Chinaye?'

Suddenly Chhering Topagyal asked Geshe Jampa.

'No, not at all Mag-pa.'

His answer was simple and straight.

'How can you remember? You were only one year old when we got married. At the time of departure from her parent's house, Chinaye had been weeping for sometime clinging to you in her arms.'

Chinaye had become alive before Chhering's eyes.

'Your sister was very moderate in speech and bashful too. All the time an innocent smile used to dance on her lips, but she was emotional also as much. She could weep over a little matter and then it took many days to console her. Her nature was just like a child. Perhaps this was the reason that she was very affectionate to children. She used to sing Chyangfi[1] songs very sweetly.'

'Was Aachaa Chinaye like Mama?'

Geshe Jampa asked to imagine his sister's face.

'Yes, not completely but almost the face-cutting was like Mama. Only there was a small black-mark just below her left eye and her colour was much more golden. She looked like a fairy when she used to a make-up herself wearing a silky girdle around her waist and a string of coral and zed on her neck, to participate in any occasion.'

---

1. Chyangfi-Tibetan folk-lore.

Chhering Topagyal's eyes seemed as if they could see the picture of Chinaye hanging on the peg of the past.

'My village was at a less distance from Chamdo. You did not see that also Jampa.'

Geshe Jampa moved his head in agreement. Once again he was listening to this story from his Mag-pa today. This was not the story of fairy-land of spiritual world but his own story, that Mag-pa could not recite in Jampa's childhood. The time also could not come at that time.

'My village was out of the way. A congested path between two huge hills joined our village. There were natural but dangerous caves both sides of the path covered with wild trees and plants. Only four or five houses were there in our village that was situated at the slope of one of those huge hills. For the first time when Chinaye came to my house with me, one could see the glimpse of fear clearly on her face while passing through this dangerous path between two hills.

'How do you people come through this path per-day? Are you not frightened?'

One day she did ask me with hesitation. I laughed at her question and said—

'I am the lion of Chamdo. Why must I be afraid of these wild animals living in these caves? And you know Jampa, I was surprised when she replied in the same manner after a few months.

That area was distressed due to the attacks of Chinese soldiers. The stories of struggles with Khampas were spread out here and there. Although I had not joined any organization till that time but there was an exhilanation inside me for which sometimes I used to go to participate in such meetings.

On that day also I came late at night. Chinaye met me at the mid-way of that cavern path. All of sudden I was perplexed. Is there any devil in the form of woman? I dared and asked, 'Who is there? Then the reply came— 'I am the lioness of Chamdo, searching my lion why has he not reached home till now?' Hundred percent this voice was of Chinaye but the face of Chinaye was not visible in darkness of night. Again I asked— 'Who are you? You Chinaye?'

She did laugh loudly.

'Now you are frightened? aren't you?'

I became angry at her courage. Controlling myself I said— 'What was the need to come here alone in this darkness of night?'

'I thought, if you can pass through this path in the night, why not me?'

She replied fearlessly.

'But you should not come out in this condition…. I mean in pregnancy period…' I was worried for her but she….she was careless of all.

'Not only this child, I'll produce five more children and make them lions of Chamdo so that your loneliness may be lessened and the population of our village also can be increased.'

Her loud laughter echoed in the silence of night. I tried to control it by keeping my palm on her mouth so that somewhere patroling soldiers nearby cannot hear her voice. Supporting in my arms I brought her home giving many instructions not to come out again from the house in such a manner. Chinaye was my weakness. Her innocence and submission to me….she was not worthy of this harsh world.'

Chhering Topagyal's voice became emotional with the tears remembering Chinaye. Geshe Jampa's eyes too filled with tears for his Aachaa Chinaye.

'What happened to Aachaa?'

With great difficulty, he could ask.

'In the same way she went out to search me once again, but I came back and she could never return. I did not find her on the way too. When I heard the sound of some shoes on that very congested path, I hid myself in the bushes. The sound went far away then I ran away towards home with my heart beating loudly. I was worried about Chinaye. Little Pasi was in her lap at that time. But both were not present in the house. I searched too much, but Pasi was found nowhere and your sister's dead body was laying in that very cave. Vultures and crows... oh..... that horrible scene... my fairy like Chinaye, everything was lost Jampa. I could recognize by her coral string.... I can't forget that terrible scene till now too.'

The tears flowing from the eyes of old Chhering began to disappear in the wrinkling of his face. Geshe Jampa also concealed his face in his hands.

After sometime Geshe Jampa stood-up slowly and taking water in a tumbler from the jug, and gave it to Mag-pa—

'Don't be impatient Mag-pa. Our sacrifices will not be useless. These sacrifices itself are making the foundation of a new Tibet.'

Nodding his head Chhering Topagyal, showed his acceptance and began to drink water.

'How long will you stay here Mag-pa?'

'At least one week. Why?'

Giving back the tumbler to Geshe Jampa he asked. At present they did not need the presence of any peon among them. They were feeling satisfaction in talking to each other. This was a meeting pertaining to self apart from the political one.

'I also want to stay with you till.... I want your affectionate shadow Mag-pa.'

Geshe Jampa again came beside him and sat on his bed.

'Will your work at Sarnath not suffer without you?'

'No, I shall give instructions by telephone. Nothing to be worried about.'

'I want to come there also sometime.'

Chhering Topagyal showed his desire and Geshe Jampa did response at once—

'Please come with me this time itself. Who knows, when this opportunity may come? I myself may live there or not?'

Geshe Jampa became serious.

'Have you decided to go to Tibet?'

Mag-pa asked.

'Yes, I think so. You will be very sad reading father's letter. He has written it from jail. Mama's memory has been lost. In such a miserable condition if I don't go there, then, how cruel a decision will this be. Above all, what do you think Mag-pa? I must go, isn't it?'

'It is a crucial moment Jampa. Sometimes there is a long gap between own feeling and political feeling. Duty for your parents is your own feeling at present. The duties that are being performed by you for the liberation of Tibet, no doubt, that is purely a political feeling. Many efforts will be done to suppress that feeling when you go there in Tibet. It may be also, that you never come back here to conduct your activities that are incomplete.'

The lines of worries were coming and going on the forehead of Chhering Topagyal.

'But in the meeting, you advised that we should try to organize our people by living there.'

'Yes, no doubt, I gave advise at that time but also understand its practical problems. Tibetans are forcibly being migrated from there so that they may be declared as in minority on their own land. This is a big diplomatic policy. Today, in Lhasa, half of the population is of non-Tibetans. To organize them is not an easy task.'

'So, what to do?'

Geshe Jampa was depressed.

'We must not lose hope. It is not so that the fire of revolution has been cooled-down there. A group of representatives was sent to Tibet by His Holiness the Dalai Lama on the invitation of China. Luckily I was also one of them. There I found a spark in Tibetans. In year 1988-89, there burst forth a big violence in Tibet and to control it Marshal-law was imposed on them. Just now in previous years, I think in 1996, there was attack of bombs also on Chinese establishments, in which, so many lives were lost. Many blameless persons were punished.

'Very recently the Human rights Commission established in America also reported about liberation of Lama Tenzin that

Tibetans are unnecessarily being tortured. Without any solid evidence Lama Tenzin was declared the guilty of bomb-blast and he was given the punishment of death but, Later, it was converted into imprisonment for life.'

Geshe Jampa quoted the news published in news papers a few days before.

'That also was on this condition that if Lama Tenzin Delek improves his conduct within two years, then his punishment will be converted into life imprisonment, otherwise not. The human Rights Commission has also affixed allegations of torturing the Tibetans, issuing its report of one hundred and eight pages. It is a kind of first step of our victory Jampa that they consider our conditions.'

Chhering Topagyal's voice was full of Zeal.

'In these circumstances the Chinese Government is moving ahead with continued steps. They are showing themselves to be liberal in Tibet also so that they can stand before the world.'

Geshe Jampa's voice was furious.

'This is the more dangerous thing. Tibet will be of Tibetans or not, this question also arises by his policies.'

Chhering Topagyal put his opinion.

'The European countries and America also are listening seriously to His Holiness the Dalai Lama in this regard. In these circumstances India must take an international initiative about the autonomy of Tibet and should develop a complete policy in context to the whole Himalayan-belt. An atmosphere must be created where the Chinese Government, Indian Government and His Holiness the Dalai Lama jointly can search out some solution for Tibet and it must be acceptable by all.'

'The most thinkable part is this also that the atomic-garbage being thrown in Tibet in a large quantity reaches India through the river Brahmaputra. There are many rivers like this. It causes environmental pollution in almost all Asian countries along with India. Apart from this, the collection of dangerous weapons in

Tibet is a great challenge for world-peace. You know Jampa that forests, mountains, rivers etc. are not only environmental things for we Tibetans but our cultural identity is associated with these natural things. The same is with our Guru Desh[1] India also. When we are cutting only a tree or diverting the natural current of a river, then we are unknowingly assassinating so many stories, customs, rituals and memories associated with that tree or river. How in Tibet, the forests are being destroyed, it indicates that the earth of Tibet will convert into a desert very soon. The pregnant ladies are forced to abort and being made barren women so that the race of Tibetans may be finished gradually. It must be stopped very soon otherwise Tibet will not remain. It may be that its name also could not be found in the history-books.'

There was restlessness in the voice of Chhering Topagyal. Geshe Jampa was watching his face silently.

'If you want to stay here, inform your office by telephone. I shall do my meditation now.'

Rising from his bed, Chhering Topagyal told him.

'Will you not go to Sarnath with me Mag-pa?'

'No Jampa, let me return from here this time. If Tathagat will wish to call me to Sarnath, He will fill the minds of all with pure feeling and we shall return to His feet to go back to Tibet.'

Chhering Topagyal moved ahead toward a small room situated at the corner of this big room.

'Yes, so I do inform to my office?'

Geshe Jampa asked like an obedient child.

'Yes, do it.'

Saying it he entered the small room to meditate. Geshe Jampa looked at the clock. It was nine O'clock. Devyani might be awaking at this time. There is no hope of anybody being in the office, he thought. Usually he felt a kind of infatuation for Devyani even by remembering her but Geshe Jampa could not have any feeling for her this time. His heart seemed to be neutral. There was not

---

1. Guru Desh- Teacher country.

any kind of attachment or attraction. His fingers began to dial the number of Devyani.

'Hello?'

'Are you Devyani……speaking?'

'Yes, myself Devyani, and you please?'

A sweet voice came from that side.

'I am Jampa, from Dharmshala.'

'Oh, sir, you?'

Devyani warbled like a bird from that side.

Geshe Jampa became unsteady for a while hearing her joyful voice but next moment he controlled himself strongly.

'See Devyani, I am staying here one week more. You have to look after there, the management of monastery too with Maai. If here is something that you can't understand, contact me on the telephone. O.K.'

He finished his talk at a time in a single breath.

'Yes, anything more?'

The warbling of her voice had lessened.

'No, nothing else. Are you well Devyani?'

He asked.

'Yes sir, I am quite well. How are you sir there?'

'Just well. Something I want to bring for you from here. What would you like?'

He asked in a formal way.

'Jee, nothing. Only your blessings and affection sir…..'

She laughed.

'Well, now I put the phone down.'

'Jee, Namaskar!

And the telephone was disconnected from that side.

Geshe Jampa put the receiver on the telephone-set and watched the fresh flowers of roses well decorated in the flower-pot. Devyani had wished him on Losar with roses of the same colour. Only Devyani had dared violating his directives till today and no one else. He was influenced by her boldness. He would take any gift for

Devyani from Dharmshala, Geshe Jampa made-up his mind. He has to stay one week more. In the meantime if he talks again on telephone, he will ask her choice. But she is so egoist that she is unable to tell him her choice. Anyway, I will purchase by myself.

Thinking about Devyani, Geshe Jampa came near window and stood there. The small and tall trees seemed like shadows in the light. The atmosphere was calm and quiet. He looked far away from the window without blinking his eyes. Mag-pa was chanting the Sutta-path inside the room—

'Iti 'pi so Bhagavā : Araham, Sammā Sambuddho,

Vijjācana – sampanno, Sugato, Lokavidu,

Anuttaro Purisadhamma Sarathi, Satthā

Deva-manussānam, Buddho, Bhagavāti.'

15

Today Devyani's mind was very much distressed. She was alone on the roof of her house in the evening. The overall circumstances made her unhappy and alone. Lama Sonam Dakpa had passed away two days before. She was shocked that night due to the heart-braking cry of Lobjang and Dava. She awakened her mother—

'Mama, it seems that Lamaji....'

Her voice was shuttering due to awakening from deep sleep and her heart-beat was so fast that it was clearly audible to own ears also. Mama awoke puzzled.

'What must be done?'

Mother was asking.

'Should I wake Deepesh?'

'Yes, to Tanchu Dhondhap and Seering also from the next room. Now I go there.'

Mother went out at once from the room.

Hearing Lobjang's pathetic weeping her heart filled with compassion. How much this lady tolerates? Thinking about Lobjang Devyani also moved towards the next-room to awaken Tanchu and Seering.

'Didi, what happened?'

Tanchu Dhondhap and Seering came out from the room.

'Perhaps Lamaji...'

Her sentence was not completed yet, Seering ran towards Lobjang's room weeping bitterly. Tanchu also followed her quickly.

Lobjang had already sent the message of serious illness of Lamaji by telephone to her step-daugther Seering and son-in-law Tanchu Dhondhap. They came three four days earlier. Lobjang had requested Devyani—

'Madam, I put you in trouble, but I can't help it. I'll be very thankful to you if you give me your one room for some days to allow my daughter and son-in-law to stay.'

Devyani was in confusion for a while that she should say 'yes' or 'no'. Who knows, how many days they will stay. Lamaji's condition was getting serious day by day. In this situation they can't go at once leaving him. But the next moment Devyani repented from her heart on her inhumane thought and she gave her acceptance to Lobjang. When Deepesh heard her decision, he burst out—

'It's the limit Didi. We must pay rent and live in hen's-house? The second room should be given in charity? It is better that we must change this house now.'

'How do you cackle Deepesh? If you have to help someone, you are saying to change the house itself? Tomorrow you will say that change the world because it also expects something from us?'

Devyani told laughingly, then, Deepesh burst out again—

'I am not cutting a joke that you are laughing so. It is not proper to live in this house now.'

Devyani did not like this attitude of Deepesh. Her laughter disappeared and voice became serious—

'It makes no difference to me whether you take a joke like a joke or not but remember one thing that there is my decision too and in my decision I am completely serious and firm.'

'If you had to heap only your decision upon us, then why you brought us with you from the village? We were far better in our village. At least we were not asked to tolerate someone's assault there.'

'What?'

It seemed to Devyani as if the ground had been taken away from under her feet. To tolerate some small arrogance of Deepesh time to time did not mean that he must talk with such impertinence. Just a few days ago, Mama had told her that Deepesh insisted on purchasing a new mobile-phone-set.

'What have you replied Mama? There is one mobile already in our house. Whenever he needs, he can use it.'

Devyani had protested politely combing her hair.

'He was saying that all his friends have a mobile except him.'

Mother spoke as if in favour of Deepesh.

'His friends may have many other things too like their own houses, cars, A.C., farm-house and so on. We have to see our limit. Cut your coat according to your cloth. I don't see any benefit in pomp and show.'

Devyani had picked up her bag to go to the office.

'When will you return?'

Mother asked in frustration.

'It will be evening. Nowadays, I have to look after some official works also. Geshe Jampaji has gone to Dharmshala. He will come within one week.'

Staying for some moment Devyani explained to Mama.

'You received his telephone-call yesterday night?'

There was another type of suspicion on mother's face.

'Yes, very much his…. He will stay one week more there and to inform it, he dialed me.'

Devyani made this clear.

'No one else is there in your institute?'

Deepesh stood coming in between them and asked. His question seemed full of poison.

'Means? What do you want to say Deepesh?'

Devyani writhed in anger.

'Same, that you understand.'

'What happened with you Deepesh? You are speaking like a misled person.'

Devyani said in frustration. She was feeling hurt.

'Not only me but in the institute also, people are talking like this. The peon, guard, clerk, everyone…?'

He was also in anger.

'Your own society itself is not above them that is why…'

Her satire was sharp.

'Now if I also would have been as qualified as you are, then, certainly high personalities could be my companions. My father's shadow removed from my head in very childhood, so, depending on other's mercy, how long I can make my society of higher class?'

His satire was not weaker than Devyani. She became angry. Chewing her words she spoke anyhow—

'You have got even that support also. Ask me. What were the circumstances when I was struggling for a service to manage bread and butter. But I never talked rudely to anyone like you.'

Almost sobbingly she moved out from the room. Mother also did not try to stop her. Perhaps her son's favour was greater for her. She could have rebuked him at once for his ill-manner before Devyani, if she had wanted, but she did not. The silence of Mama at that time pinched Devyani till now. How the persons were going far away from her, for whom, she was devoting her every moment one by one.

Devyani took a long breath and with a sigh walked on the roof slowly. Today she was unable to control her emotions. Eyes were filled with tears again and again. The loneliness and despondency made her heart restless. The sun had set behind the cluster of trees. The Chaukhandi Stupa[1] looked like a shadow. This famous monument was popular as 'Seeta Rasoinya'[2] in the local people. Many times a curiosity rose in Devyani's mind— Why and when the name of Seeta would have been associated with this particular place? Nowhere in history, it was written. It was known by hearsay that Ram and Seeta stayed here for sometime while in exile. Several times Devyani wished to go to this place and see it but she could not go there living in Sarnath itself. When Geshe Jampa returned this time she will ask him the history of this place.

Next moment, she herself laughed at her foolishness. How Geshe Jampa can tell the history of that incident related to Mother Seeta. The person, who himself is struggling to save his history and

1. Chaukhandi Stupa-A famous monument at Sarnath.
2. Seeta Rasoniya-Kitchen of Goddess Seeta, wife of Lord Ram.

culture, what can he tell me about the ancient mythological and historical truth of India?

Devyani forgot the previous bitterness as she remembered Geshe Jampa and was reminded of how she should inform him about the death of Lama Sonam Dakpa and the illness of Maai Dolma caused by that shock. Moreover, Geshe Jampa must be informed about the activities of the institute also. She looked at her wrist-watch in the street-light. It was seven O'clock in the evening. She dialed his number on her mobile-phone. All of sudden Devyani thought that this information is no reason to talk to him. These are not so important that he must be informed at once. It can be narrated when he comes back. It maybe that Geshe Jampa would misunderstand her. She put the switch off and started walking out of restlessness.

She was again reminded of the dialogue with Deepesh. What would the guard have told him? Once she had come back to the present the flowers on the occasion of Losar. That guard was watching her with astonished eyes. It seemed as if she was doing something wrong. Many times Geshe Jampa himself calls her. He does not let her leave without taking tea. When that guard used to come with tea, she had seen a doubt floating in his eyes to see her in the chamber of Geshe Jampa, but she always overlooked it. Who knows, that very guard himself had cackled about the relation of Geshe Jampa and her. Oh, we women, may anything be, posted on higher chairs, be of any age group, we can't be deprived of being a mere woman. Our being a women is a heavier burden that weakens us too. We are always afraid of being woman with its attribute because that is the easiest place to make a social assault.

Murmuring by heart, as Devyani moved ahead towards the ladder to go down from the roof, the mobile rang suddenly. She saw the number on the screen and a small light of happiness sparkle in her heart. It was Geshe Jampa on the mobile phone. She returned on the roof. The sound is received clearly in open area, she thought.

'Jee?'

She told in place of hello. Her voice was trembling out of excitement.

'Hello, Devyani?'

Again was asked from that side.

'Jee, I am speaking.'

Her voice became sweeter with respect for him.

'Had you given me a telephone-call just now?'

'Jee, sir, I had to inform you about something that has happened here.'

'Then, why did you disconnect it?'

'Jee, I first thought that it could be told after your return also. You will worry there.'

'Anything special?'

He asked.

'Jee, Maai is ill. Actually, my house-owner Sonam Dakpa, younger brother of Maai….he passed away two days ago….'

'Oh!'

Geshe Jampa's voice sank in grief.

'Take care of her Devyani. She is old. This shock….'

Devyani interrupted and said—

'Jee, you don't worry sir. I visit her daily.'

'I trust you Devyani.'

An affectionate emotion overflew in Geshe Jampa's tone. Devyani's palm began to perspire. She took mobile in her other hand.

'You are saying nothing Devyani.'

'Jee, I am speaking.'

'That, I can't hear.'

His soft laughter again overflew and scattered around the ear of Devyani.

'Jee, there were some official matters too that I'll tell you after your return here.'

'Why? Why not just now?'

'Jee, you have gone there for some other important work. These official problems are not so important that you should feel tension there.'

'What happened? Tell me Devyani. I have seen so many and such types of problems in my life that these small things do not effect me.'

Devyani felt a kind of agony in his tone. She started to tell him—

'Sir, the senior clerk and Mahipal, the sweeper, they quarreled very badly one day. Perhaps Mahipal had given some money to the senior clerk as a bribe to pass his medical-bill. But the work could not be done and both started blaming each other. Mahipal was declaring loudly that he had given him a bribe and the senior clerk was denying therefore. A kind of drama was going on in the office for sometime and the people were enjoying like onlookers. Anyhow myself and Mr. Thapaliyal could subside the matter.'

'What do you think, who is right in your opinion?'

Geshe Jampa asked suddenly.

'It seemed sir that Mahipal was right. But he is also a culprit because, he gave a bribe in the first place to get his work done and afterwards he was shouting about it…. He is no less a sinner….'

She gave her decision.

'O.K. I am coming after three or four days, then I'll look into the matter. And, how are you people? I have talked so much and did not ask about you. You will think, how selfish am I?'

The soft laughter of Geshe Jampa from that side made of Devyani blush. She held the mobile-set with both hands.

'Oh, no sir. Not so. 'She replied with hesitation.

'How is the wife of Lama Sonam Dakpa? I'll come to meet her.'

'Jee, she is in deep grief.'

'It is obvious. May Lord Buddha give her peace of mind. Watching these sorrows of the world asceticism took place in His heart.'

Geshe Jampa became philosophic.

'But everyone can't kick the world like Tathagat. Some attachments are such that grip the feet of a person.'

When Devyani also put her opinion, Geshe Jampa again laughed slowly.

'I like your becoming logical and argumentative with me in every matter. Here I would say, that the all bindings that could fasten the feet of Tathagat were with Him also. But he had to go and he went too. Bindings were broken, attachment vanished and he attained the pure knowledge. Today the whole world is enlightened by this knowledge.'

'I don't agree sir. Excuse me, if I hurt your feeling. This decision was one-sided, and that was not proper at all.'

'If he would have been contemplating on both sides, perhaps he again might be allured.'

'No, inspite of this harsh decision, it would have been better that he should have discussed with Yashodhara[1] and would have left in her knowledge. Yashodhara would not have felt agony so much.'

'It might be that her grief would have increased more and then Siddharth could reserve his decision. I do not condemn the woman-race, but she is so delicate a creation of nature that sometimes she becomes the weakness of a man and thus, an obstruction too.'

'No sir, I very humbly disagree with you. There is a lady who is considered as hindrance due to her emotional and soft attachment and on the other hand, the Kheer[2]of a lady's hands becomes the light of the path of knowledge. What you can say to this aspect of a woman's life?'

'This was the reason Devyani for which Lord Buddha had to return once to Yashodhara after attaining the knowledge.'

---

1. Yashodhara-Wife of Lord Gautam Buddha.
2. Kheer-A dish made of rice, milk and sugar boiled together. A Lady Sujata had given the 'Kheer' to Lord Buddha and after that Buddha attained His enlightenment.

'But, He could not return those moments to Yashodhara that were filled with agony due to Him.'

'Who can fill the sorrowful moments with joy Devyani? What to say about men, even deities also are unable. No power has been created till now who can reverse the cycle of Mahakal[1]. This cycle is pushing us ahead and ahead every moment. Tathagat was also not beyond that supreme power. Neither you or I.'

'............' Devyani was silent.

'Why did you become silent?'

The serious voice of Geshe Jampa sounded on the phone.

'My logic has no response to this sir.'

She spoke slowly.

'So many things are beyond logic and are purely the subject of feelings. Increase your power to feel. Concentrate your heart in someone and then describe to me your feelings of it. It is a very pleasant thing.'

'Sir, pardon me for my audacity. At present are you concentrated in your spiritual upliftment or in service of your nation?'

'In both, Devyani.'

'Is it possible sir?'

'Both are related to each other at some juncture.'

'Then only love is not related with the life?'

There was silence for a moment. Devyani thought it better to clear her meaning.

'From love, I mean son, wife, parents or there may be anyone. One can attain his goal with love also. I think love is not an obstruction but it works as a medium to attain the goal. Women must not be considered as a weakness, but she can be treated as energy and this is the right way.'

'Now I am defeated by your logic. I know that you don't want to be a loser. Your logic is unrevokable. I think now, we are talking for a long time. I must break. See you soon.'

'Jee, good night.'

---

1.   Mahakal-Supreme power of cosmos.

A delicate pride mixed with sweetness overflew in her tone. The phones were disconnected from both sides.

As soon as Devyani turned back, she saw her mother standing on the stairs. She was astonished for a moment. Mother was listening to her for a long time.

'Was this phone-call of your Geshe Jampa?'

Mother asked abruptly. Her tone was full of doubts.

Devyani did not feel good. Controlling herself she replied—

'Yes, it was his.'

'How long is it proper to talk about love with a monk? Is he also doing dissimulation behind asceticism?'

Mother's voice was aggressive. Devyani tried to convince her—

'Mama, actually we are in the habit of taking only one meaning of love and we can't think beyond it. This is the reason that you are also talking in such a way. I was discussing with him the life-style and philosophy of lord Buddha and you caught a word 'love' firmly and kept it on the hill of wastes. It is not proper mama to think like this about me or him.'

'To whom and whom I must tell proper or improper about you? To Deepesh, to our neighbours, or to myself?'

Mother burst out.

'Then, what should I do? Should I leave the job? Should I not talk to anybody because I am a woman?'

Devyani also was annoyed.

'Do your job as all do. Talk to everyone but in such a manner that no one can get a chance to think or doubt for something else.'

Mother became polite. Devyani also realized her fault. All the circumstances were enough for anybody to suspect. To talk on the roof in the darkness of night anyone could take another meaning without knowing the reference of the discussion.

'You are so innocent mama. Sometimes there is a long distance between ear and eyes. Whatever one hears is not truth and the real truth can't be seen.'

She caught her mama in her arms.

'Come, mama. I prepare a very tasty tea for you. Come!'

She helped her mama to come down the ladder.

'My daughter! Have only those dreams in your eyes that can be true in real life too.'

Mother again warned her.

'Oh mama! You imagine far and far away.'

Devyani became serious. Mama's warning brought her far away very often in the night and again left her in the lap of the ocean like tired waves return. Was there any dream really creeping into her heart? She was groping in the dark.

16

Geshe Jampa was walking in his chamber in restlessness. It had passed three weeks since his return from Dharmashala. In this period he was in extreme confusion. He could not take any final decision on the letter sent to him by his father from Tibet. While his departure from Dharmashala, Mag-pa made him to understand in warning tone—

'See Jampa, take any decision carefully. Any step taken in hurry may be dangerous for your future. It also may be that this letter is a fraud.'

'Yes Mag-pa, I am also thinking in this direction since then. A stirring is constantly going on in my mind. Now I have got your support too. I'll contact you before I reach my final conclusion.'

'I should dial you as soon as I reach Kembra. You will have arrived at Sarnath by that time.'

Mag-pa said keeping his air-bag on the bed. His flight was in the evening. It took very less time to pack his luggage.

'Yes Mag-pa, I shall reach Sarnath by tomorrow. If you also come with me, I would feel happy.'

Mag-pa diverted his topic—

'When you go to Tibet, visit my village too anyhow. How is Chamdo now, write me.'

There was a thirst craving in Mag-pa's eyes for his village.

'You also try to reach there Mag-pa. I shall feel loneliness there.'

'Hush! How you talk like a child. Own earth, own sky, memories of our own people, all will be with you there. How loneliness? Talk to the clay of Nang-gar-che. Embrace hills and valleys there. Ask the whereabouts of the wind. Then search into your heart that, is there someone to be remembered? Nobody will be reminded there, Jampa. Yes, remember only one thing, that is your mission, and that will go with you from India.'

Mag-pa was speaking and being emotional. Geshe Jampa was listening to him carefully. In his mind, Sarnath was stirring, that will perhaps go with him to Tibet, along with its racial reminiscenes and all its peculiarities.

'Are you lost somewhere Jampa?'

Mag-pa asked him.

'No, Mag-pa. I think, how man is helpless in the cycle of the world. These discrepancies became our destiny because of living on a particular piece of land. Neither destiny nor a piece of land could be changed?'

'Are you disheartened by the prevailing circumstances?'

Mag-pa put his affectionate hand on his head.

'No Mag-pa, only I am contemplating on it.'

'Then think on this point too that on which land you are standing now that is called India, did it not face such circumstances? After the incarnation of the Thathagat on this land, it has seen so many ebbs and flow which are written in history now. We are also making an effort to make the history of Tibet. You are associated with the land of knowledge and the first preaching of lord Buddha. Why is there such delusion in your mind? Why is the darkness enhancing?'

Mag-pa's hand was still on his head.

'When a twinkling lamp in the gust of wing gets the palm-shade on it, then the complete light of lamp is focused only on the palm and the other side remains only dark. This time your protection is just like that.'

'Have patience Jampa, everything will be alright.'

Mag-pa had embraced him. There were tears of departure in the eyes of both.

'As I think, it will be better, that you wait at present Jampa. Let the another letter come from Tibet, then decide to go there.'

Mag-pa told him by contemplating something. His voice was emotional now.

'But till then mama and father…. .'

He was confounded.

'Whatever may be accepted by god Avalokiteshwer…...'

And only after three weeks of his arrival from Dharmashala Geshe Jampa received another letter. He opened the letter with trembling fingers. The writing seemed to be of father. To confirm it, he hurriedly drew the previous one from the almirah. The hand-writing of both letters were same. There was a haziness before his eyes. Wiping his eyes with the corner of his Cheevar, he began to read it—

Dear Jampa,

Unlimited blessings!

'Time is going on. Hope is being converted in distress. Perhaps you will not come. I don't know, how long I am going to survive. I want to see you only once. Your mother is trying her best to save her few breathes so that she can see you. I think, she must leave the world now because if there are hope of survival for few days too but in such type of hell, then it is better to detach from those breathes also. She has reached the same state of detachment. What is rest for her? Only I, a pitiable skeleton. Chinaye was lost, Kon-Chog was also lost. You were cursed to depart. Nothing was known about Mag-pa. Why should we survive and in which hope? And moreover in this prison? Every morning is miserable, every evening praying for mercy…... . Perhaps these miseries would have been lessened if you come back.

But you Perhaps…... ..'

Your Father

Thupten.

Geshe Jampa's eyes were filled with tears. How helpless his father was? The mark of a cross after the incomplete last line of the letter was stirring him in confusion. Father will not have made this mark without any intention. Perhaps that mark was made by him to forbid Jampa from coming Tibet or it may be the symbol of his hopelessness for this rest of the life. It may be also that this mark was symbolic to write a letter under pressure of someone.

Confounded Geshe Jampa dialed the number of Mag-pa in Kembra—

'Mag-pa, again there is a letter from father.'

'Oh,…. is writing his own?'

Mag-pa was also puzzled.

'Yes, Mag-pa, I can recognize the hand-writing. It is hundred percent of my father himself. I tallied it also.'

'What has been written in it?'

Mag-pa's tone was full of worries.

'Full of hopelessness. Not a single ray of hope for life is there with father. Only depression and frustration.'

'What do you think Jampa? It is his own expression or under any pressure….?'

'The expressions full of sorrow seems to be his own but there is mark of a cross at the last line of the letter, that is very emotional and incomplete too. I am trying to derive the meaning of that mark since the letter has been received. I thought, your suggestion might solve the problem in this direction.

'Hum…. what do you think?'

Mag-pa asked.

'Mag-pa, I do think that this letter has been written under the pressure of someone. The mark of the cross is made to forbid me from coming Tibet. But in my opinion, I must go there now. After all, as you instruct me.'

'I also think so Jampa. You must go now. Is there something written about me also? Are we also remembered or not?'

There arose a curiosity in Mag-pa's heart.

'It is written Mag-pa. He has written with much grief that, Chinaye was lost, Kon-chog also was lost and nothing is known about Mag-pa too.'

'Really, has he written about me too?'

There was a child, like joyful sound in Mag-pa's voice.

'Yes Mag-pa, it is written.'

'Oh, how this misfortune is that we departed from our country, cursed to be far away from our parents too and now if we have to go back to Tibet even, then, in so many impudent and hypocritical conditions.'

His tone became serious.

'You had told me Mag-pa that we are creating our new history and today you are being weak yourself? I am going there soon. Will you also come?' Geshe Jampa asked him.

'My good wishes are with you Jampa. I'll try my best to come there as soon as I get the opportunity. Be alert there. Your activities will be watched there. A small carelessness can hit our mission. Be in less contact with me. It must be better that we exchange our messages with the help of any mediator.'

Mag-pa had made him alert.

'Yes, Mag-pa. But that mediator will be of Kembra or here?'

'Knowing the name of Kembra, the spies will follow us and they will search out the relation between you and I. If someone may be very faithful in Sarnath to whom I and you, both can write a letter, then it will be better. He can convert my information in his own words…. no one will guess that really whose message it is? Is there someone so faithful to you? Only to take precaution, I think so.'

Mag-pa was asking on telephone and Geshe Jampa's mind wandered everywhere and stayed with the name of Devyani.

Today he called Devyani in his chamber to meet him after revealing the name of Devyani to Mag-pa on telephone. In the meantime he looked at his watch from time to time. There was a restlessness in his heart while walking in his chamber. What will Devyani think? Her gift was kept in almirah brought by him from Dharmashala but he could not dare to give her because of these confusions and hesitation also. Today he wanted to present it.

To purchase it he had entered a handicraft shop in Dharmashala. He took this decision after thinking on it a lot. He did not know the likings of Devyani. Moreover, he was hesitant in purchasing ornaments or clothes related to a woman. What the shopkeeper will think watching a monk purchase it. And above all, Devyani may also think something else. A painting based on any ancient Indian myth will be better as a gift for her, he thought.

The Shopkeeper had shown many paintings in Kangra style. In some, there were the references related to the life of Lord Ram and Seeta and in some the fully-overwhelmed postures of Radha and Krishna. Being very attractive too, he diverted his eyes from those paintings. To present it to Devyani also may give bilateral meaning. All of sudden his eyes stayed on a painting in which a beautiful lady was sitting alone amidst alluring nature. The lotus-flowers were blooming in the pond before her. Bent headed and keeping one hand on her knee, the lady also held a lotus in her other hand. Sunk in thought her eyes seemed as if they were asking something from the pond. The transparent upper garment covering her bodice was expanded aside on the earth, and the corner of it was shown caught in the mouth of a small deer as if that deer was making the lady aware of its presence. A sage coming out from the cluster of shrubs behind that lady, had held his wooden spout in one hand and the index finger of his other hand was raised out of anger.

'What is the story of this painting?'

Geshe Jampa asked the shopkeeper.

'Jee, it is based on the story of Shankuntala and Dushyant. This scene is related to the malediction of Durvasa.'

The shopkeeper explained it cleaning the painting with a cloth.

'Hum, can you give its literature also?'

He asked with curiosity. The shopkeeper laughed.

'Swamiji,[1] everybody knows this story. The name 'Bharat'[2] of our country is also on the name of Bharat, the son of Shakuntala.... this great lady.'

---

1. Swamiji-An address to a saint.
2. Bharat-The original name of India.

The shopkeeper explained indicating towards that cursed-lady in the painting.

'That is why I want to read it.'

'I don't have this literature swamiji. You purchase the book Abhijyan Shakuntalam of Mahakavi Kalidas[1] with Hindi annotation from any book-shop. You might not be knowing Samskrit but you can read its Hindi annotation.'

The shopkeeper had solved his problem.

Geshe Jampa came back purchasing that painting. He was satisfied and happy also that he had got a nice gift to present Devyani.

Devyani will be pleased to see it.

'Sir, may I come in?'

All of sudden the voice of Devyani had made him astonished. He snapped back from the past and came into the present.

'Yes, yes, come in Devyani. I was waiting for you.'

His voice was very quiet but soft.

'Something new sir?'

She was also curious. After questioning, her eyes started wandering here and there. Now a days without any clear reason she was avoiding his sight.

'Be seated. We can have a cup of tea.'

He said while sitting on his chair.

'I don't feel the need of tea sir, but if it is your order then....'

She did laugh gently. This was her third meeting with Geshe Jampa after his coming from Dharmshala. The first time she came to meet him with the staff. The second time, he met her in Maai Dolma's room unknowingly. He went there to see Maai after his arrival from Dharmshala. Devyani also used to go there almost daily after taking her class. Usually the topic of their discussion was either of Maai's past or the struggle of Lobjang and Sonam Dakpa.

'Then, my order is this that we must talk while sipping tea.'

---

1. Kalidas-A great Samskrit poet of India.

Geshe Jampa told with a feeling of togetherness.

Devyani liked it. Her lips trembled in acceptance.

'Will you take something with tea?'

'Oh no sir.'

She said this with an effort. Geshe Jampa pushed the call-bell silently and ordered the guard to bring tea. In between the time there was a mysterious silence spread out in the chamber. Devyani used to look him often. Geshe Jampa was revolving the paper-weight slowly catching with his hands. Lost in contemplation one could easily guess that he was in deep thought.

This silence seemed unnatural to Devyani. she interrupted quietly—

'Sir, today you look more worried. What is the matter? If I am worthy to know it...'

She left her sentence incomplete.

'Aahn, yes. Really I am very worried. I stand on such a turning point from where it is not very easy to take any decision.'

Devyani's heart did beat fast. God knows what is the matter? She put her silent question by curving her eye brows.

'I'll tell you Devyani. Also I need your suggestion and opinion. I can't succeed alone in defeating the dialectical situations, Devyani.'

Geshe Jampa's eyes were focused on Devyani.

Devyani felt as if her ears and cheeks were red with warmth. She pretended to wipe it from the corner of her Saree.

The guard came with tea. Devyani did overcome for some moment from that feeling of embarrasement but watching that guard her face became colourless for a moment. She was reminded of Deepesh. The warning of Mama also flashed into her memory. All the emotions were a jumbled mass. She felt abnormal. To control herself she at once held her cup of tea and started to take a sip. When she looked towards Geshe Jampa, he was watching her attentively. The cup of tea was kept as it was, before him.

'Oh, please excuse me sir, I started first.'

She was filled with hesitation.

'It doesn't matter Devyani. I am seeing that you are more puzzled than me. What is the matter? If it can be solved by any one. I am ready to do it.'

'No sir, nothing like this. Sometimes unwanted thoughts roam here and there in one's mind. A man always lives either in the past or in the future. He can stay only for few minutes in the present.'

She laughed.

'Yes, that is why he is seer of dreams. Dreams are only with human beings. Perhaps the world of animals is not gifted with this precious thing. As they have nothing except their present, so dreams are also far away from them.'

'Who knows sir, may be that they see. They don't have the medium of expression, perhaps for this reason we don't know or hear about their dreams. A philosopher had said that man has imagined his God in the form of man. If an ass or monkey could have the medium of expression, then, their God would be like them.'

'You have beautiful logic Devyani. You have studied a lot.'

Geshe Jampa was influenced by her.

'Thank you Sir, I am grateful for this appreciation.'

She was hesitant.

'First of all, I must give you your gift .'

Geshe Jampa tried to rise from his chair.

'My gift?' She became puzzled.

'Yes, it is yours. I don't know if you like it?'

Now Geshe Jampa was slightly hesitant. Bringing out a packed painting from the almirah he came and stood near Devyani. She also stood from her chair in hurry.

'What is this sir?'

Her tone was mixed with joy and astonishment.

'You yourself open it and see.'

Giving the packet in her hand, he himself sat there on sofa beside her. Devyani was opening the packet with hesitation and he was watching ebb and flow on her face.

'I could not know Devyani what to buy for you from Dharmshala. After thinking a lot I chose this painting. Do you like it?'

'Jee, very very much. It's a very beautiful painting.'

'A cursed lady.'

Geshe Jampa took a deep breath.

'Jee, but I think it was necessary for her to be cursed in order to save Dushyant's character.'

Devyani sat on her chair beside him keeping the painting in her lap.

'What do you mean by that Devyani?'

Geshe Jampa displaced his curiosity. He was less aware of this story.

'Perhaps you might be knowing sir, that this scene is related to sage Durvasa's Curse of Shakuntala. If this episode of curse would not have been associated with the story of Shakuntla and Dushyant, then Shakuntala remained the heroine of this story as she was, but the character of Dushyant could have become a villain— a trivial personality, cheating the emotions of an innocent lady. But this curse episode made-over his character. To make Dushyant superior, Shankuntala made her life cursed.'

'Hum.'

He could speak a little listening to her carefully.

The discussion once again stopped. A silence spread out in the chamber and the waves of this silence were touching them in their own way. Devyani was looking at the painting and Geshe Jampa's eyes were concentrated on the calendar hanging on the wall. The guard had gone taking the empty cups.

'Devyani, next week I am going.'

Geshe Jampa broke the silence and Devyani became astonished.

'Where?'

'Tibet.'

'What.....'

Her reply carried into the distance.

'Yes Devyani, I have to go. A letter has come from there. My father is alive till now.'

A glimpse of happiness flashed in his tone like a child.

'Congratulation sir, But before it….?'

Devyani stopped herself from asking something.

'Yes, yes, you can ask Devyani. Before it, nothing was known about him. Since the time, when I left Tibet, till today nothing was known about him. I sent letters many times but no reply came from there. How could he get my letter? He was imprisoned for so many years.'

He became serious.

'Oh, why in jail sir?'

'For Tibetans living in Tibet, it has become a common thing. If someone is suspicious, send him or her in jail with some pretence. If he has participated in any movement, send him inside.'

'This is completely unfair. It is a violation of human rights sir. A voice must be raised against it.'

'It is raising Devyani, but the result is not up to the mark. To destroy our activities they are trying their best. Now look at me, I could not hear about the torture of my parents. I consoled myself for so many years in the state of not getting any whereabouts of my parents, but all of a sudden, by receiving this letter I am perplexed. It may be that their emissary-agencies would have given them information about me and they might be using my parents as weapon to call me back. By torturing them, this letter has been written by them so that I must come. Anything may happen, this is why my parents had not written to me for so many years living in jail? Certainly it is the evil deed of the administration. They might have collected informations about me.'

Geshe Jampa was explaining and Devyani seriously listened to him.

'Then, you will go?'

The anxiety of her tone was not hidden from Geshe Jampa. He watched her without blinking his eyes for sometime and replied—

'I have to go.'

'When will you return?'

'I don't know. Maybe, never.'

His eyes were still focused on Devyani.

Devyani bowed her eyes and began to look at the painting. Her heart was restless in an unknown agony that she did not want to expose before him.

'You too always used to say that one can't fight for one's freedom living abroad. One must enter the current of the river in order to know it.'

Geshe Jampa provoked her with sad smile.

'Then sir…. I had not told for this. I meant….'

There was a sorrow in her demeanor.

'I do not take your words otherwise Devyani. Don't feel sorry for it. Only I need support from you again. Will you do that?'

'Please tell me sir.'

Her large eyelashes bowed blinking.

'Will you agree if I send any letter to your address and I want that message of my letter to be sent by you from your side to Kembra, the address of which I shall give you?'

'I do not understand sir.'

'My elder brother-in-law Chhering Topagyal lives in Kembra. He gives me fatherly affection. Only you have to become a bridge between him and I.'

'Jee, as you say.'

She became uneasy.

'I am not talking today as your senior officer. Now you are totally free from that feeling. At present, I, a Tibetan citizen, requesting for co-operation from a great Indian lady. Will you co-operate with me?'

'Why do you ashame me sir? Can I refuse you?'

'I had faith in you previously and today that faith has been confirmed.'

Being sentimental Geshe Jampa put his hand on the right palm of Devyani and held it firmly. Both were sitting for some moments in torpor. The next moment Geshe Jampa became conscious when he felt the slow trembling of Devyani's palm filled with hesitation and he hastily withdrew his hand from her hand as if he had committed something wrong.

'Oh, please excuse me Devyani, it was an emotional outburst…'

He could not speak further.

'Jee, I can understand. No matter Sir. Don't think it.'

But Devyani's cheeks were flushed. To control her uneasy breathes she clung both her palms together.

Geshe Jampa stood-up. A glimpse of hesitation was clearly visible on his face.

'Is there no possibility of coming back or to stay here sir?'

She made an effort to wipe up his guilt.

'Now it depends on the circumstances Devyani. Your love and co-operation will be our support there too.'

He went to his chair and sat bent-headed. A heavy silence spread-out in the chamber. After a long silence he raised his head and watching Devyani said seriously.

'Now, you may go Devyani.'

She was very sad. Her eyes were ready to overflow.

I'll start from here for Dharmashala on Wednesday evening after three days from today, and shall go to Tibet, my own country from there, itself.'

There was neither happiness nor agony in his voice, only a neutral emotion that anyone could guess.

'Tashi Delek sir.' Hardly she could say and turned.

Clinging the cursed-lady to her heart she went out from the room with heavy steps. A sight twisting between love and detachment had come to drop her out from the door.

17

The very next day this news spread among the local Tibetans' community like a fire in the forest that in order to stop the religious and political activities of Geshe Jampa and also to create fear in Tibetan refugees, he is being called-back. To make this happen, they have made a weapon out of his old parents and they were forced mentally and physically by torture to write that letter. As soon as Geshe Jampa gave his official charge to other officer, the monks and students of the Tibetan Research Institute and monastery started to be gathering before Geshe Jampa's office. Tanchu Dhondhap and Lobjang also got information from Devyani. Under the leadership of Tanchu Dhondhap, a symbolic silent procession of protest had gone to the Chinese temple situated at Sarnath from the Tibetan temple and converted into a public meeting before coming back to the office of Geshe Jampa.

The high priest of the Chinese temple said with politeness—

'I can understand your feeling. I myself want to become the central sandstone amidst the flood of unrest. If you can trust me, I'll also send an appeal from my side. They have to chose one, either Lord Buddha and his peace or war. They have to make it clear now that whether they like peace or violence. For peace, compassion is the first step but their actions don't give the reflection of it. Have faith in me, I will appeal from your side too. I am with you. The compassion of Lord Tahagat is with you. Everything will be good.'

Tanchu Dhondhap had handed-over the letter of the non-violent-movement and reproach letter to the high priest in which the diplomacy of the Chinese Government to call-back the active members like Geshe Jampa was condemned. A photo-stat copy was at once sent by Fax to the government of India and the other embassies. Taking a decision to send a copy of it to Human

Rights Commission, the procession came back to the office of Geshe Jampa. Chanting the slogans against the exploitation by the Chinese Government which they held in their hands the students and monks became emotional as soon as they reached the office of Geshe Jampa—

'Geshe Jampa, don't go back…. Don't go back…. China stop your diplomatic politics… Stop your duplicity.'

The slogans were being chanted out by loud-speaker in front of his office. Hearing the noise Geshe Jampa was perplexed. He did not expect that there may be an agitation on the issue of his going back to Tibet. He came out from his chamber with folded hands out of politeness. He also became emotional watching the public sentiments for him.

'See, your love will support me there. We must go there if they call us by diplomacy itself. We are leading our movement for a long time living far away from our country but the proper result could not come yet. So, please do not stop me from going there.'

'Then you will not go alone Gela. We shall be with you. We'll go with you.'

They shouted. Hundreds of hands swayed in the air. The students were aggressive. The faces of monks were also excited. Standing behind the crowd, the lady monk Dolma was watching everything with distressed eyes.

'Look, that moment has not come at present. I hope that time will come very soon when we shall celebrate Losar in Potala together. Only you give me your support and maintain your morale.'

Geshe Jampa requested.

'If there would have been misbehaviour with you then?'

Tanchu Dhondhap was in anger.

Now days he was living in Sarnath with Lobjang.

'I don't think that they will do so. Yet, we must be ready to face anything. Such type of religious-annihilation, cultural-annihilation and genocide is not found in any world-history to finish a race. If we are victims of such brutal exploitation then we must be ready to face everything too.'

×   ×   ×   ×

Next day, the crowd, that had come to see him off at the railway station, heaped him with garlands and flowers.

The faces of monks and students were filled with sorrow and excitement and above all that with the very feeling of being called refugees. Geshe Jampa's eyes were filled with tears again and again. He was saying goodbye to each by stroking or touching the shoulder with affection or shaking hands. The senior clerk of the institute came ahead with Balendu and Naveen Sharma holding a big garland of flowers—

'Sir, please don't forget us. Come back soon.'

Naveen Sharma became emotional. Without uttering a single world, Geshe Jampa embraced him in his arms and tapped him on his back. Balendu also came near to him. Geshe Jampa embraced him also and spoke in an emotional voice—

'Look after the children and the institute carefully after me. Don't let Maai Dolma feel lonely.'

'Yes sir.'

Tears were in his eyes too.

The train had whistled. Geshe Jampa stayed a short and looked everywhere in search of Devyani.

'Has Devyani not come?' His voice was trembling with emotion.

'No sir.' Balendu replied.

And Geshe Jampa turned to go towards his compartment in a gloomy mood. The sun was going to set in front of him.

Date of Birth: 15th March 1962
Place of Birth: Village - Kotwalpur,
Post- Muftiganj , District -Jaunpur, Uttar Pradesh

Parents: Mr. Mathura Prasad and Mrs. Vimla Devi
Husband's name- Dr. Beni Madhav

Neerja Madhav is a distinguished Indian author who has written over 53 books, including acclaimed novels such as Denpa: Diary of Tibet, Geshe Jampa, Tebhyah Swadha (The Bite of the Partition of India), Yamdeep, Tashkent Uttargatha, Anupamey Shankar, #Corona, Avarn Mahila Constable ki Diary, Tripura , Ratrikalin Sansad, Riding the Tiger : A Research Scholar's Diary etc _ Her literary contributions span across genres-novels, poetry, short stories, and essays.

Her poetry collections include Pyaar Lantana Chahega, Likhate Huye Shokgeet, Save the Earth, and Free Tibet. She has also written on critical social and national themes in works like Arthat Rashtravad, Bharat ka Sanskritik Swabhav, and Hindi Sahitya ka Ojhal Nari Itihaas, addressing issues such as Kashmir, nationalism, Tibetan rights, Indo-China border dispute as well as third-gender identities in Bharat, Traditions of Shankaracharya and history of Hindi literature.

Her creative writings are featured in the curricula of several universities in India and abroad. For her outstanding contribution to literature on Tibet and world peace, she received the Nari Shakti Puraskar 2021, India's highest civilian award for women, from the Honorable President of India Mr. Ram Nath Kovind_ She was also honored with the M.P_ Sahitya Academy Award for Geshe Jampa, Dr. Hedgewar Pragya Samman (2021), Maithili Sharan Gupt National Award for 2023 and the Sahitya Bhushan Award from UP Hindi Sansthan, Lucknow.

Neerja Madhav has been conferred the honorary title of Sahitya Mahopadhyay by the Prayag Hindi Sahitya Sammelan. She was invited to Canada to deliver lectures on Indian culture and human values, where she was honored by the Legislative Assembly of Alberta.

Contact: Madhuwan, SA 14/96 N-5, Sarangnath Colony, Sarnath,
Varanasi- 221007, Uttar Pradesh, India
Mobile +91 979241 1451, +9182991 89766
Email: neerjamadhav@gmail.com

BLACK EAGLE BOOKS

www.blackeaglebooks.org
info@blackeaglebooks.org

Black Eagle Books, an independent publisher, was founded as a nonprofit organization in April, 2019. It is our mission to connect and engage the Indian diaspora and the world at large with the best of works of world literature published on a collaborative platform, with special emphasis on foregrounding Contemporary Classics and New Writing.